CHAOS AT CHRISTMAS

When Ferelith's family-run hotel is taken over by a billionaire, plus his friends and relations, no one could have predicted the colourful mayhem that ensues for the hardworking staff. But between soothing egos, investigating possible crimes, running impromptu parties and picking up fake snow, will Ferelith have time to let gorgeous head gardener Geraint know how she feels about him?

EWAN SMITH

CHAOS AT CHRISTMAS

Complete and Unabridged

LINFORD
Leicester

First published in Great Britain in 2021 by
D.C. Thomson & Co. Ltd.
Dundee

First Linford Edition
published 2023
by arrangement with
the author and
D.C. Thomson & Co. Ltd.
Dundee

A catalogue record for this book is available
from the British Library.

ISBN 978–1–4448–5182–3

Published by
Ulverscroft Limited
Anstey, Leicestershire

Printed and bound in Great Britain by
T.J. Books Ltd., Padstow, Cornwall

1

'Ferelith, might I ask a favour?'

'Yes, of course, Monsieur Berthier. How may I help you?'

He held her gaze for a moment, a lock of his jet-black hair falling across one eye.

'It's Laurence, I've told you,' he murmured.

Ferelith maintained her polite expression but she didn't respond. The policy at Fosbury Manor was clear. Staff at the hotel never addressed guests by their first names; there were standards to be upheld.

Laurence Berthier stretched out a languid hand and took a sip of his espresso. Ferelith's eye was caught by his chunky gold signet ring inset with a glowing dark stone. Just as it had been caught by the hand-made shoes, the lichen-green suit, the perfectly knotted tie and, above all, the waistcoat. Its colours were exquisite, like the sky at dawn.

'After my parents and I have Christ-massed here at Fosbury Manor, I'm jetting off to Canada for a few weeks to stay with my uncle and aunt at their Ontario estate.'

Ferelith smiled. 'How lovely.' In the New Year, she would be returning to her cramped student flat which she shared with three friends. That would be lovely too, in rather a different way.

'My cousin has promised to take me ice-fishing.' He looked at her with a frown. 'Could you arrange for someone to give me a tutorial?'

Ferelith blinked. 'A tutorial on ice-fishing?'

He nodded. 'Just to cover the basics. I don't want to look a fool when I go out with Étienne. This afternoon would be perfect.'

She nodded slowly. 'Certainly, Monsieur Berthier. I'll look into that and get right back to you.'

He smiled at her and she wondered if he practised doing that in front of a mirror; he had such gorgeous film-star looks. His phone made a melodious sound and he pressed it to his ear.

'Isha darling, hello,' he murmured. He waved a hand at Ferelith vaguely. She had been dismissed.

★ ★ ★

Lionel looked at her in amusement. 'Young Monsieur Berthier wants a tutorial on ice-fishing?'

Ferelith nodded at her father. 'I don't quite know what to do. It's not something that's been covered on my course.' She was studying for a degree in hotel management.

'That's an outrageous omission; you should complain.' Lionel smiled. He gazed out of the window and Ferelith followed his eyes. That morning she had seen Geraint, the young head gardener, clambering about the ancient oak tree. Thanks to his efforts, it was now draped with Christmas lights which swirled with glowing colours. 'Monsieur Berthier must have his tutorial. At Fosbury Manor, what our guests want . . .'

'. . . our guests get,' Ferelith automatically responded. It was the mantra which the staff at the Manor had drummed into them relentlessly. Under Lionel's management, the hotel had developed an unrivalled reputation for personal service.

He swung back in his chair. 'The Canadian Embassy — you should contact them. They must know someone who knows about ice-fishing.'

'Of course. I'll get right onto it.'

'How are things going for you anyway?' her father asked as she turned to leave.

Her eyes widened with pleasure.

'I'm enjoying every minute of it.'

During the three weeks of her university break, she was working at Fosbury Manor as a general assistant. Her help was certainly needed. Every room at the Manor was booked by guests eager to share in the hotel's renowned festive celebrations.

4

Lionel frowned. 'I feel a bit guilty persuading you to work here when you should be enjoying your Christmas holiday.'

Ferelith put her arms round his neck and kissed him warmly on the cheek.

'I love working at the Manor, Dad. It's such brilliant experience for my course. I'm having to do so many different kinds of things.'

'Such as arranging ice-fishing tutorials?'

She laughed. 'Exactly. I'd better get on with it.'

As she made her way across the marble floor of the reception hall, she felt a deep sense of satisfaction. It was such an elegant space, decorated so beautifully for Christmas. The previous afternoon, she had helped Jane Soutar, the chief housekeeper, dress the imposing tree which now twinkled magically in one corner. She listened to the hum of conversation from the guests scattered around the comfortable armchairs as the staff moved quietly about serving coffees and pastries.

At times, she felt as if the hotel was a beautifully intricate machine whose parts never worked less than perfectly. There was Jane the housekeeper, of course, and Erik on the front desk; Madame Pomfret who looked after the dining room; Konrad Schuster in the exercise suite; Geraint the head gardener and dozens of others. The staff at the Manor all took such pride in their work and in the service they provided to the guests.

She stopped by the reception desk. Erik was listening with great patience as an elderly lady guest explained how the tiny dog in her arms was a creature of extraordinary intelligence.

'I truly believe that she can understand every word that I say. Isn't that right, Charlotta?' She and Erik gazed at Charlotta, who ignored them. 'Of course, she is very discriminating in her responses . . .'

Erik glanced momentarily at Ferelith. His eyes informed her in the politest of ways that members of the hotel staff didn't stand in front of the reception desk, that area was reserved for guests alone. Ferelith slipped behind the desk as the elderly lady wandered off and Erik smiled at her. 'What can I do for you, Miss Ferelith?'

'I need a computer, Erik. Is there one I can use where I won't be getting in anyone's way?'

'Of course. There's a laptop in the security room behind us. Would that suffice?'

'Excellent.'

The security room was empty with a quiet hum coming from the screens filling one wall. She sat down at the desk. 'Right then,' she murmured. 'The Canadian Embassy.'

It was the sort of task she loved. There had to be dozens of people working at the embassy, maybe hundreds. Surely someone among them was a keen ice-fisher? All she had to do was track that person down. Having found the number, she called the embassy and explained her requirements.

The man who answered was polite but firm.

'I'm afraid that's not that's not something we can assist you with. Have you tried Yellow Pages?'

Ferelith wasn't put off. 'Perhaps someone in your tourism department could help?'

Moments later, she was being overwhelmed by a gush of warmth and enthusiasm.

'Canada has so much to offer the visitor. It's one of the most beautiful countries in the world, full of picturesque forests, mountains, and lakes. If you like camping, hiking, or just wandering around admiring the views,it is the perfect holiday destination. Then there are our winter sports like skiing, snowboarding and snowshoeing. You'll find such a wealth of excitement in . . .'

'Ice-fishing!' Ferelith said, bursting into the torrent of words. 'It's ice-fishing that I'm particularly interested in.'

The woman paused for a moment.

'To be honest, ice-fishing isn't one of

our major tourist draws.'

'I'm looking for someone at the embassy who would be willing to give a one-to-one tutorial on the subject.' Ferelith hesitated. 'This afternoon.'

There was a longer pause.

'I'm afraid that no one springs to mind.'

'Perhaps there's someone else who might be able to help?'

Over the next half hour or so, Ferelith became familiar with the many different departments of the Canadian Embassy. No one she spoke to seemed able to help but she made sure that she was always passed on to someone else. She was sure that there had to be a keen ice-fisher somewhere in the building. Then she hit the jackpot. 'Is that the Department Of Agriculture And Development?'

'No, ma'am. This is the embassy kitchen.'

Ferelith frowned. Had that nice woman in the Visa Office passed her on to someone else at random just to get rid of her?

'I don't suppose you know anything about ice-fishing?'

'Nothing at all, I'm afraid.' Ferelith's shoulders drooped. 'But I know someone who does.'

Ferelith's eyes widened. 'You do?'

The woman was shouting. 'Pascal. Pascal!' She returned to Ferelith. 'Pascal, one of our porters, is mad keen on ice-fishing. Here he is.'

A friendly voice began speaking into the phone.

'Hey there, this is Pascal Clermont.'

She explained the situation. 'Our guest just wants someone to share the basics of ice-fishing with him.'

'I'd be very happy to do that,' he said eagerly. 'It's the one thing I miss about living in London. Ice-fishing is the best sport in the world.'

That brought Ferelith up short. She couldn't imagine what fun there was to be found in holding a tiny fishing rod over a small hole in a frozen lake for hours on end. But she pushed that thought out of her head. 'It has to be this afternoon.'

'Oooff,' Pascal said in a vague noise of French-Canadian uncertainty. 'That could be a problem. My shift at the embassy finishes soon but I have a lot on this afternoon.'

Ferelith tried to inject some rampant gorgeousness into her voice. 'I'd be so grateful to you, Pascal,' she murmured huskily.

Rather to her amazement, it seemed to work.

'I suppose I could rearrange things,' he said reluctantly. 'How about if I got together with your guest on Skype? I could manage that.'

Ferelith knew that Laurence Berthier had been thinking of a person-to-person meeting but this might be as good an offer as he was going to get.

'I'll see what he says, Pascal, and get right back to you.'

As she passed behind the reception desk, she noticed that Erik seemed to be dealing with someone who was booking out, which struck her as odd. However, her mind was on other matters. She found Laurence deep in conversation with his parents.

'My apologies for interrupting you, Monsieur Berthier, but I have someone who would be happy to give you an ice-fishing seminar this afternoon. Would you mind if it took place on Skype?'

'Good heavens, no. I want to see him in person so he can demonstrate the techniques properly.'

'It's just that . . .'

His handsome forehead creased with a frown.

'I had hoped that this would have been sorted by now, Ferelith. Something has come up. Time may not be on our side.'

Ferelith heard her father's voice in her head. *What our guests want, our guests get.*

She stifled a sigh. 'Of course, Monsieur Berthier. I shall arrange the matter at once.'

She hurriedly retraced her steps. Now there was a crowd of people gathered around the reception desk. And more of them seemed to be booking out.

'Miss Ferelith, can you give us a hand?'

Erik hissed at her in passing.

She grimaced an apology. 'Sorry, Erik, I'm on a mission.'

Back in the security room, she called Pascal back. 'I'm afraid that the seminar will have to be one-to-one. Could you come here to the hotel?'

He made another French-Canadian noise. 'I don't think that will be possible.'

It seemed he was starting to go cold on the idea but Ferelith suddenly realised that there was something she hadn't yet mentioned. 'You'll be paid for your trouble, of course.'

There was a silence. 'How much?'

His voice sounded more interested, though Ferelith had no idea what she should offer.

'A hundred pounds?' she suggested.

'Agreed,' he replied immediately. 'I'll have to reorganise my afternoon but then I'll come straight to you.'

Ferelith sat back in her chair, feeling drained but pleased. It hadn't been easy but she'd got the job done. At the reception desk, there was now a noisy throng

13

of people clamouring to be dealt with. To her surprise, she spotted Laurence and his parents amongst them.

'Good news, Monsieur Berthier. Your ice-fishing seminar is all arranged.'

He shook his head. 'I can't manage that now. We're leaving.'

Ferelith's mouth sagged open. 'Leaving?'

'Erik, did you arrange a taxi?' Laurence called.

'It'll be outside in two minutes, Monsieur Berthier.'

'Marvellous.'

Ferelith couldn't believe it. 'But, Monsieur Berthier . . .'

However, Laurence Berthier wasn't listening. 'On y va, Papa, Maman,' he said and, with a wave of the hand, he was gone.

'Erik, what on earth is happening?' Ferelith said in confusion.

'I wish I knew.' For once, he sounded rattled. 'People are leaving the Manor and moving to other hotels on the spur of the moment. I've never seen anything like it.'

'What people?'

'Guests. Dozens of them. The whole hotel is emptying.'

'I don't understand.'

At that moment, her phone rang. When Ferelith saw the name on the display, her shoulders sank. She forced a smile onto her face. 'Pascal, hi.'

'I've managed it, Ferelith,' he said, sounding very pleased with himself. 'It wasn't easy but I've rearranged everything. I'm on my way!'

She closed her eyes with a groan.

2

'Of course, madam. I'll have your Bentley fetched from the garage immediately. It will be waiting for you by the front door.'

'And my luggage?'

'One of our porters is on his way to your room to collect it even as we speak.'

That wasn't absolutely true but, with a bit of luck, it would be very soon. Ferelith waved a hand to attract Erik but his attention was being taken up by an elegant couple who had both been talking to him at once in rapid Italian.

'Non è affatto un problema, signora, signore,' he said with a smile that seemed to have become fixed to his face.

The voice on the phone broke into her thoughts. 'Tell your porter to hurry. I don't want to be kept waiting.'

'Of course not, madam. He'll be with you shortly.' Ferelith crossed her fingers as she said that and the Italian couple finally turned to leave.

'Erik!' she hissed at him. 'We need a porter at room 104. Pronto!' His shoulders sagged slightly.

'I'll contact Madame Pomfret. We'll have to use the waiters.'

Ferelith gazed at him in shock. The waiters at Fosbury Manor were the finest in the business. Some of them had worked in prestigious hotels all over Europe. It was unthinkable that they should be asked to lug suitcases around.

Erik saw her expression.

'We have no choice; the porters are being run off their feet. I've already roped in Geraint and the ground staff to help.'

Ferelith's ears pricked up as they always did when Geraint was mentioned. She barely knew him, but she was hoping to change that situation very soon. Recently, she had found herself being constantly distracted by thoughts of his curly brown hair which never quite stayed in place and his habit of buttoning up his waistcoat wrongly which she found so sweet.

Then there were his hands, which sometimes got a bit grubby from his work. She longed to moisten them with a damp sponge and rub them gently but firmly with the lemon-scented soap someone had given her the previous Christmas. Once they were perfectly clean, she would take them in her own hands and press them to . . .

'Ferelith!'

Her attention was hauled back to the present. 'Yes, Erik?' she said, feeling strangely breathless.

He indicated with his head. 'The phones?'

Five lights were flashing on the panel in front of her; it was an unheard-of situation. At the Manor, guests were never kept waiting. She hurriedly pressed one of the buttons and glanced at the display showing the customer details. 'Mr Leigh-Humphreys, how may I help you?'

Her phone call with Pascal earlier had been awkward in the extreme. He had gone to a great deal of trouble to rearrange his afternoon, only for her to tell him that he was no longer needed. It was fair to say that he wasn't best pleased. She had decided to avoid the area of London around the Canadian Embassy for the next few months to minimise the risk of bumping into him.

However, seeing that she was free, Erik had immediately grabbed her. It was never possible to say that there was chaos at Fosbury Manor; it was a hotel run with supreme efficiency. However, the system had definitely begun to creak at the edges as countless guests suddenly announced that they were leaving the Manor and moving to other hotels. Reception had become a mass of people demanding attention.

'Could you help answer the room calls?' he had said to Ferelith. So she had sat with two other members of the reception staff and dealt with call after call after call.

Time passed in a blur. Guests at the Manor expected an immediate response to requests for service and they were all requiring attention at the same time. It felt to Ferelith as if every member of the hotel staff had been roped in to cope with the situation. At one point, she spotted Geraint hurrying through the reception hall with a guest's luggage. There and then, she made an early New Year's resolution. Sometime in the next twenty-four hours, she would find a chance to introduce herself to him properly. The prospect was like a little beacon of light which kept her going through the endless succession of calls.

'Yes, Ms Hendron-Wyse, our chief laundress is very familiar with designer underwear. She will have the items collected, laundered and forwarded to your new hotel straightaway . . .'

'Of course, sir. Caviar, sushi and an organic lamb burger for Room 31 as a snack before the three of you leave . . .'

'I will despatch someone to our Nordic spa immediately to look for your missing sock . . .'

'A bottle of glacier water, Sir Gervais?

Of course. Arctic or Antarctic?'

An endless time seemed to pass before Ferelith finished a call and found that none of the lights in front of her were flashing any longer. For a moment, she wondered if the panel had developed a fault. But then she realised that, miracle of miracles, it was because there were no more guests requiring attention.

She sat back in her seat with a groan. Her ear felt twice its normal size, her brain ached mightily and she thought that she would prefer not to have to deal with the demands of hotel guests ever again for as long as she lived.

'Thank you for your help, Miss Ferelith,' Erik said, seeing she was off the phone. 'We pride ourselves at the Manor on being a place where we all pull together. But I don't think I've ever seen it put into practice quite like that before.'

Ferelith glanced round the reception hall. The people standing about in small groups were members of the hotel staff. The guests all seemed to have gone.

'You have been magnificent,' Erik

called out. 'I thank you from the bottom of my heart.'

They began to clap; there were a few cheers.

'I still don't understand what's been happening,' Ferelith said in puzzlement.

Erik shook his head.

'I have no idea. In a matter of hours, we have become a hotel without guests.'

'They've all gone?'

'Not a single one left.'

'But this is our busiest time of the year.' He held out his hands in a shrug.

'Excuse me, everyone, could I have your attention?' Ferelith turned. It was her father. 'Staff meeting in the main conference room now. For everyone, please. As quickly as you can.'

Ferelith considered hurrying over and asking him what on earth was going on. But something held her back; she didn't want to take advantage of her position. The other members of staff were no doubt just as keen as she was to find out what was happening.

As everyone started making their way

to the conference room, she spotted Geraint with a group of people a little way ahead of her. She realised that it was the perfect opportunity. Accelerating smoothly, she caught up with them.

Of course, they were discussing why all the guests had left.

'Could there be a sickness bug going round?' someone suggested. 'You hear of cruise liners being cleared of passengers due to illness.'

There was a dismissive snort.

'Have you noticed that Fosbury Manor isn't sailing the high seas?'

'Anyway, this isn't a case of guests having to leave; they all chose to do so themselves.'

'And they were transferring to other hotels. Why would anyone prefer somewhere else to the Manor?'

'Maybe our reputation is slipping?'

'Apparently some guests said that they were leaving because all their bills at their new hotels were going to be paid for them.'

'That's true,' Ferelith said. 'A couple

told me they were off to have a brilliant Christmas at the Saint Regis and without paying a penny for it.'

Geraint turned to her with interest. 'Really?'

Ferelith's heart began to race. Her chance to speak to him had come much sooner than she had expected. She nodded eagerly.

'It seems strange, but . . .'

But there was an interruption.

'Geraint, do you have a moment? I wanted a quick word about fresh flowers for the dinner tables.' It was Madame Pomfret, who was in charge of the dining room.

Geraint smiled. 'Of course, Eugenia,' he said, drifting away from the group to speak to her.

Ferelith's eyes narrowed. She had always admired Madame Pomfret but it occurred to her that it was possible to go off people.

'I want to thank you all so much. This afternoon, you did a fine job in very unexpected circumstances.' Lionel gazed at the staff gathered about the reception room. 'Though it's no more than I would have expected. At Fosbury Manor, we are above all a team.' There were murmurs of agreement. 'However, I'm sure that you're wondering exactly what has been going on. I wondered that myself when I started getting reports from Erik on the front desk that our guests were leaving en masse.

'The fact is that Fosbury Manor is now an empty hotel. However, that's not something for us to worry about because, this time tomorrow, we will be full again.' Everyone began to listen intently. 'I don't know if any of you are familiar with the name Lyle Cranford.'

Ferelith had heard the name but couldn't place it. Was he an actor, maybe, or a sports star?

'Isn't he the internet millionaire who invented FastChat?' one of the porters called out.

Lionel nodded. 'Absolutely right apart from one small detail. Lyle Cranford isn't a millionaire, he's a billionaire.

FastChat has become one of the most popular social networking services in the world.'

Erik frowned. 'I believe he has the reputation of being something of an eccentric.'

'It's a reputation that's well-earned,' Lionel retorted. 'He was the person responsible for emptying our hotel today. It seems that his people contacted every single guest of ours and invited them to move immediately to one of a selection of other five-star hotels. If they did so, all their bills would be paid, not only from here but also from the other hotels. They wouldn't have to spend a penny on Christmas.'

'That'll cost him a fortune.'

'Indeed, it will. Luckily for him, he has a number of fortunes at his disposal.'

'But why did he want all the guests out of here?' someone asked. 'Does he have a grudge against us?'

'On the contrary, he wants Fosbury Manor for his own Christmas celebrations. For the next week our hotel will be full of his family and friends.'

There was a stunned silence.

'As you can tell, he is a man with money to spare who likes to indulge his fancies. But tomorrow morning, the Manor will start filling up with guests again. So we had better prepare ourselves to receive them.'

The staff scattered with an eager buzz of conversation.

'That's rather unexpected news, Dad,' Ferelith said to her father. 'It sounds as if Christmas at the Manor is going to be a bit different this year.'

'That's certainly true. I suppose it might be a good opportunity for the hotel. Someone like Lyle Cranford could bring us a whole new clientele.'

'That's great.' She noticed the look on her father's face. 'Isn't it?'

Lionel had taken a sheet of paper from his pocket and was reading it with a troubled expression.

'Just before I called this meeting, I received an email from Franklyn Boscoby; he's Lyle Cranford's personal assistant. He sent a list of 'a few small things' which Mr Cranford wishes to have attended to. You won't believe some of the items he's got down here.' Lionel shook his head. 'I suspect that we are going to have to work very hard to earn our pennies this Christmas.'

3

It was bedlam, that was the only possible description. Normally, a grand piano in one corner of the reception hall was played for an hour or two every day. It helped create the harmonious atmosphere which so characterised Fosbury Manor.

However, that morning, Miss Buckley-Tone's gentle music was drowned out completely by chatter and laughter and squeals from children running around. The new guests had arrived.

The trouble was that they had all turned up at once. Also, most of them knew each other. So instead of the normal quiet hum at reception, there was a chaotic racket going on.

Erik seemed stunned by the turmoil.

'Is there anything I can do?' Ferelith asked.

It was an unprecedented situation. All eighty-six rooms at the Manor had become empty at the same time which meant a huge job of cleaning and preparation for the household staff. What's more, the list of new guests had only arrived by email that morning so the allocation of rooms was having to be done in a rush. And, normally, things were never done in a rush at the Manor.

He gripped Ferelith's arm with a glazed expression. 'The children — please do something about the children.'

There were dozens of them chasing each other around the reception area, all full of the Christmas spirit. Two girls rushed up to the desk.

'Is our room ready, Mum?' one asked eagerly.

Her mother smiled. 'Not yet, darling. But I'm sure that it won't be long.'

The other girl clambered onto the desk. Picking up the handbell there, she started singing *Jingle Bells* at the top of her voice using the bell as a rhythm accompaniment.

Ferelith thought Erik might be about to spontaneously combust. The bell was a purely ceremonial item. Staff at the reception desk never needed to be summoned; they were always available. Her mind raced.

'Girls, would you like to play some games?' she said brightly.

The girl on the desk stopped singing. She and her sister looked at each other. 'We might do.'

Trying not to notice Erik's astonishment, Ferelith pulled over a chair and climbed onto the desk herself. She winked at the girl and nodded towards the handbell. 'Give it some welly.'

Delight spread across the girl's face. Grasping the bell in both hands, she began ringing it as loudly as she could. The noise reverberated round the hall and Ferelith glimpsed her father gazing at her open-mouthed.

She put a hand on the girl's arm. The ringing died away, leaving only the sound of Miss Buckley-Tone playing *Silent Night* on the piano with her usual delicacy.

Everyone had turned to look at

Ferelith; the guests in amusement, the staff with horror. She wondered if she had just said goodbye to her temporary post at the hotel.

'Children,' she called cheerfully. 'It's going to take a little while for your mums and dads to find out which room you're in. In the meantime, you're all welcome to come with me to . . .' Ferelith hurriedly considered the options. 'To the sports hall, where we'll have some games.'

There was an interested murmur.

'There will be refreshments,' she added.

'Will there be banana sandwiches?' someone called out.

Ferelith stuck up a thumb. 'That happens to be our chef's speciality.'

There was a cheer and children began hurrying towards her. She climbed down off the desk.

'Sorry about that, Erik.'

'Don't apologise,' he retorted fervently. 'If you get the children out of the way then at least we'll be able to think. And don't worry about the refreshments;

I'll sort them out.'

Ferelith turned to the young musician. 'Are you ready to rumble?'

The girl nodded and, accompanied by the deafening ringing of the handbell, Ferelith led the way followed by an eager gaggle of youngsters.

★ ★ ★

The next hour or so passed in a blur. There must have been thirty or forty children and all of them were up for fun. They played Follow The Leader, Stick In The Mud and Freeze Tag. They danced the *Macarena*, the Hokey Cokey and the Conga. They sang *Gangnam Style*, *YMCA* and *Baby Shark* and then some of the girls taught everyone else how to Time Warp. By the time three groaning refreshment trolleys were rolled into the sports hall, Ferelith was ready to lie down in a dark room with an ice pack on her forehead and stay there until Easter.

Fortunately, as the rooms became organised, the children were gradually collected by their parents. In the end, the only ones left were Holly and Bree, the two sisters who had started it all.

'Haven't your parents got your rooms yet?' Ferelith said. 'Let's find out what's going on.'

Holly picked up a mini-doughnut oozing cream and chocolate sauce from the trolley.

'We got our room ages ago. But we told our mum and dad that we wanted to stay.'

'Can we do this every day?' Bree asked eagerly. 'It was fun.'

Ferelith's smile stiffened a little. 'We'll see.'

★ ★ ★

Back in the reception hall, things had returned to the Manor's normal state of calm efficiency. Guests were scattered around the armchairs chatting and laughing together but no one was waiting to be dealt with at the desk.

'I'm afraid that the sports hall is in a

bit of a mess, Erik,' Ferelith said uncertainly. 'A food fight broke out at one point.'

But he just held up his hands.

'That isn't a problem. Clearing away messes is a simple matter; dealing with hordes of over-excited children is something else altogether. I'm enormously grateful to you.'

Lionel appeared at their side.

'Is everything all right?'

'It is now,' Erik retorted. 'I was just explaining to Miss Ferelith that, by removing those children from the hall, she rescued me from a fate worse than death.'

Lionel glanced at Ferelith in amusement.

'I did wonder when I saw you climbing onto the desk if the stress had got too much for you.'

Ferelith grimaced. 'It wasn't really the Manor's way of doing things, was it?'

'It was quick thinking on your part. And that's going to be needed over the next ten days. This could be a Christmas unlike any other.'

'It certainly looks that way,' Erik said with feeling. 'I've been told some of the guests have started swapping rooms. They're treating the Manor like a family home, not a luxury hotel.'

Lionel smiled. 'I'm sure we'll cope. We just have to try to be flexible.'

Erik didn't seem convinced. 'I'm fifty-seven years old. My flexible days are behind me.'

'Shall we have a coffee?' Lionel suggested to Ferelith, leading her away. 'As it happens, that's something I wanted to get your views on.'

Ferelith looked at him in confusion.

'About being flexible?'

He shook his head. 'About giving the Manor the feel of a family home. With our new cohort of guests, that's actually what we want this week.'

They stopped by the Christmas tree. Ferelith noticed the expression on her father's face.

'Is there a problem?'

'It's beautifully decorated,' Lionel

murmured. 'But it is quite formal. I wonder if we could make it look more like a family Christmas tree.'

Ferelith thought for a moment.

'How about personalised baubles? I saw some on Pinterest the other day; wooden decorations with laser-cut messages. We could have separate baubles with each guest's name on them.'

'That would be perfect.'

'I'll get onto it. Though it might cost a bit.'

Lionel shook his head. 'Don't worry about that; cost isn't an issue when it comes to Lyle Cranford.' He frowned. 'Though I was also thinking about our big Christmas Eve celebration. With so many children and young people staying, we need to make it more of a family party. I wonder if we should have a visit from Santa Claus?'

'I had a thought about that. I spoke to Carola Ricci earlier, she's the set designer at the local theatre. She said that if we made a donation to their Christmas charity then she would be willing to turn one of our reception rooms into a Christmas grotto. It should look amazing.

'I also spoke to Dandy Barham, one of the Ugly Sisters in their panto. He would be happy to dress up as Santa and hand out presents at the party.' A rueful look crossed her face. 'Though he made it clear that he would like to be paid in cash.'

'But that would be fantastic. We should absolutely go ahead with both of those ideas.' He looked at Ferelith thoughtfully. 'You're doing good work for us.'

Ferelith grinned.

'I'm having the time of my life, Dad.'

A thin middle-aged man in a dark suit bustled up. 'Mr Gwestyr? I'm Franklyn Boscoby. We've been in touch via email.'

'Ah yes — you're Lyle Cranford's assistant.'

Franklyn's eyes flashed. 'Chief of staff.'

Lionel smiled at that. 'This is my daughter, Ferelith. You could say that she's acting as my chief of staff this Christmas.'

He ignored the remark and pointed at

the tree.

'This will have to go.'

Lionel blinked. 'What?'

'Mr Cranford has an abiding concern for the environment. When it comes to Christmas trees, he insists on live ones in their own pots.'

'But our head gardener went to a lot of trouble to get this tree,' Ferelith protested.

He looked at her coldly. 'Then he can go to a little more trouble to find an environmentally friendly replacement.'

Ferelith turned. But it was clear from her father's expression that Franklyn Boscoby would have his way. If Lyle Cranford wanted a Christmas tree in a pot, that was what he was going to get.

She made her way miserably out into the grounds. She had wanted to introduce herself properly to Geraint, but not like this. She was the bearer of bad news and, all too often, they became associated with their message.

She found him by the lily pond with two members of his staff, manoeuvring into place a large log on which people could sit and enjoy the peace. She stood and watched for a moment. He had his coat off, sleeves rolled up, with muscles in all the places muscles were supposed to be. It occurred to her that, if there was a sudden emergency and he had to sweep her off her feet, he would manage it without any trouble at all.

She imagined the scene; her lying in his arms, him gazing down at her, a lock of his hair falling across his forehead which she reached up to...

'Can I help?'

Ferelith gulped. 'Hi ... yes ...' she said hoarsely.

He was looking at her with such a friendly smile. It made her a little dizzy, though in a good way. But then she remembered the message she was bringing and her excitement drained away.

'I'm afraid I have some bad news.' She told him about Franklyn Boscoby's demand.

Geraint gazed at her in disbelief.

'He wants us to replace a tree of that

40

size this close to Christmas?' Ferelith grimaced. 'I'm sorry.' He struggled not to give vent to his feelings. In the end, he made a sound somewhere between a sigh and a groan. 'I'll see what I can do.'

Ferelith felt grateful; she had expected him to make more of a fuss. But that made the next bit of news even more difficult to pass on.

'There is something else as well.'

Geraint's eyes narrowed. 'What?'

'He's also planning to have the grounds of the hotel covered with artificial snow.'

4

'I don't see the problem. I emailed you the details of how the dining room is to be organised.' Franklyn Boscoby sounded terse. Ferelith suspected that he didn't much like having his instructions queried.

'I just wanted to be clear about Mr Cranford's wishes,' she said in her most emollient tones. 'He would like separate tables for breakfast . . .'

'With plenty of room between them. People aren't necessarily in the mood for chat and jollity first thing.'

'Then at lunchtime, the guests are to sit in tables of eight . . .'

'Mr Cranford believes that people interact most effectively in groups that size.'

'Ri–ight.' Ferelith wasn't entirely convinced but she didn't intend to get involved in a discussion on the matter. 'And for dinner . . .'

'The tables should be in a large circle with the guests facing inwards. Then if someone wishes to address the whole group, they can do so from the centre.'

That someone being Lyle Cranford, no doubt, Ferelith thought.

'Thank you, Mr Boscoby, that's very clear. I do appreciate . . .'

But he had already turned to leave. She gave a faint sigh. The dining room staff were about to have a great big problem dumped in their laps.

* * *

Madame Pomfret gazed at the proposed table arrangements. 'I may keep these?' she said, indicating the printouts.

'Of course, Madame.' Ferelith felt rather intimidated. Madame Pomfret ruled the dining room with immense authority, and the standards she set for both herself and those around her were of the very highest. 'I realise that reorganising the dining room for every meal will mean a lot of extra work for your staff, but . . .'

But Madame Pomfret had lifted a finger.

'It is not a problem. If it is what Monsieur Cranford wants . . .'

'. . . then it is what Monsieur Cranford gets,' Ferelith retorted with an uncertain smile. 'But how will you manage things at dinner? The tables aren't designed to fit in a circle.'

Madame Pomfret's shoulders gave the faintest of shrugs. 'I will deal with it.' She spoke as if the problem hadn't yet been invented which she couldn't solve.

'Thank you, Madame. Thank you so much.'

'Good day, Mademoiselle Ferelith.'

Ferelith felt relieved as she left the dining room. The encounter hadn't been as bad as she had feared. She hurried back to her temporary office in the security room. Her father had asked her to sort out the cleaning rota and she was finding it a tricky task. With the hotel being full, all kinds of demands were going to be made on the cleaners. However, many of them had young families themselves and had asked for some time off over Christmas.

She brought up the spreadsheet on the laptop. But just as she began to study it, the phone at her side rang. It was her father.

'Sorry, Ferelith, but could you pop down to the exercise suite? Konrad has some sort of problem with the Christmas arrangements for the pool.'

'OK, Dad. I'm on my way.' She closed the spreadsheet again with a sigh and got to her feet.

★ ★ ★

The hotel's exercise suite included a gym, sauna facilities and an extensive pool area. It was overseen by Konrad Schuster, a cheerful titan who had once been a member of the German Olympic bobsleigh team.

'My total apologies, Ferelith, but I do not know what to do.' He held out a set of printouts and Ferelith's heart sank.

She recognised the FastChat logo. 'I have received many instructions from a Herr Boscoby . . .'

Ferelith nodded. 'Lyle Cranford's assistant.'

'Herr Cranford wish for blow-up desert island in swimming pool for the children to play on. I think such a thing impossible but, to my surprise, I manage to hire one so that is okey-dokey. He also want supply of special water-gun to be available. In normal time, this is absolutely against the rule in our pool. But since we are having private party in the hotel I agree to their use. However, I must buy these water-gun at much expense.'

'Don't worry about that,' Ferelith assured him. 'The bill will be passed on to Mr Cranford.'

'However, my true difficulty is with third requirement. Herr Cranford wish for sand pit in pool area.' Konrad held out his hands. 'Look around. We have exercise pool, play pool, spa pool, paddling pool. No room for sand pit.'

Ferelith gazed about. He was right. On the other hand, the hotel had its reputation to uphold. Her eyes suddenly narrowed. She nodded to the small circular spa pool.

'What about closing that temporarily and filling it with sand instead?'

Konrad thought for a moment, lips pursed.

'Ye-es, that might work. I could fit rubber liner to protect spa pool.' He grimaced. 'Of course, sand will get everywhere. And it will be devil of job to clear up once Herr Cranford's guests leave.' He stood, hands on hips, thinking. Then he nodded. 'But yes, I believe that will do the task.' He grabbed Ferelith's hand and shook it enthusiastically. 'Good work, Ferelith. Problem solved.'

Ferelith was soon in front of the laptop again and opening up the cleaning spreadsheet. But before she even had a chance to look at it, her phone was vibrating.

She groaned; she just knew that it would be another problem involving

Franklyn Boscoby. She lifted the phone to her ear.

'Hi Dad.'

'Could I see you, Ferelith? Something has come up.'

Franklyn Boscoby was waiting impatiently in her father's office.

'Mr Cranford has contacted me to say that he will be arriving this afternoon.'

'That's what we expected, isn't it?'

'And he'll be coming by reindeer sleigh.'

Ferelith's mouth sagged open.

'He'll be bringing pre-Christmas presents for all his guests and he would like everyone assembled on the front lawn to greet him. However, he wants to make sure that the grounds are covered with the artificial snow before his arrival.'

Ferelith was struggling to grasp the concept of 'pre-Christmas presents'. But she pushed that to the back of her mind.

'About the artificial snow,' she began.

'A special effects company will be arriving...' Franklyn glanced at his watch. '...some time in the next hour to deliver it. Of course, the snow is made from biodegradable paper and is 100% environmentally friendly.'

'But the grounds are looking so beautiful.'

He shrugged carelessly. 'And they'll look even more beautiful covered in snow.'

His phone began to chirrup and, without another word, he turned and strode away. Ferelith gazed at her father.

'Is this fair on Geraint and his team? They have worked so hard getting the grounds ready for Christmas.'

Lionel lifted his hands. 'I appreciate that. But if it's what Lyle Cranford wants . . .'

Ferelith nodded. 'I'll let Geraint know that it's on its way.'

However, she found she had missed him. Faisal, one of the under-gardeners, told her he had gone to collect the replacement tree.

Her eyes widened. 'That's fast work.'

Faisal grinned. 'Geraint doesn't hang around.' But all at once, the smile fell from his face. 'What on earth . . .'

A huge lorry had turned through the entrance to the hotel grounds and was nosing its way up the drive. Ferelith gazed in disbelief as it came to a stop by the front door with a deafening shriek of its brakes. On its side, there was a gaudy 'Spectacular FX' sign surrounded by erupting volcanoes, collapsing buildings, exploding planets and a scantily dressed young woman screaming with all her might. It wasn't the sort of image that the Manor would wish to present to its guests.

'You can't park here,' she protested to the driver. 'Trade vehicles have to go round the back.'

He shrugged. 'If you want artificial snow at the front of your hotel, then this parks at the front.'

To her relief, she saw her father hurrying out to join them. After a brief but heated discussion, the driver climbed back into his cab and moved the lorry round to the side of the building.

The three-man team got to work.

They pulled an extendable tube out of the rear of the lorry. Two of the men held on tightly to the end of it as a rumbling motor started up. They were like firemen with a hose, except that this hose was considerably bigger.

'Stand back, everyone,' one of them yelled. 'Winter is coming!'

A spray of white began pouring from the hose. It rose into the air in an arc then scattered and drifted to the ground like real snowflakes. The men began walking slowly across the lawn, turning the hose from side to side. Ferelith picked up a handful of the artificial snow. It was made from tiny strips of very thin paper rolled into pea-sized balls. All around her, the ground was becoming covered in a layer of white. A few guests had wandered out of the hotel and were watching with curiosity. Two children began jumping around in the snow and kicking it into the air.

Lionel hurried forward. 'Children, for your own safety, please stand right back,' he called out.

One of the men raised a hand.

'Don't worry, mate. They're fine so long as they keep away from the hose.' He turned the nozzle and directed a spray of the snow into the air above the children. They shrieked in delight. Within moments, others joined them and the lawn became the scene of an impromptu party. As the two men gradually covered the ground at the front of the hotel, even some adults started to join in the fun.

'This is so much better than real snow,' one laughed. He was lying on the ground waving his arms and legs to try and make a snow angel. 'It's not cold and wet.'

Ferelith watched with concern as more people gathered and the party grew noisier.

'Shouldn't we stop this, Dad?'

Lionel grimaced. 'I'm not sure I can. Anyway, our guests are having a good time — isn't that the whole purpose of them staying at the Manor?' He looked around. 'And the artificial snow is effective. We're starting to look more Christmassy.'

It was true, Ferelith thought, though she suspected that it might not look so festive once it was trampled into the ground.

'Perhaps I'll arrange for the kitchen to do some hot chocolate and nibbles. That might go down well with the younger guests.' He brought out his phone and keyed in a number.

It was amazing how quickly the men finished the job. Soon, the grounds at the front and sides of the hotel were covered in white and the equipment was being packed away. It was a complicated business getting such a large lorry reversed and turned, and everyone had to be cleared out of the way. But then, with an entirely unnecessary honk of its horn, it headed off down the drive and away. Within moments, the snow party was under way again.

A group of shrieking children raced past, throwing handfuls of the artificial snow at each other. Ferelith gazed after them in dismay. They were running all over the flower beds. She hated to think of the damage that was being done. After all the hard work done by Geraint and his ground staff, the plants were going to be ruined.

5

Ferelith took a sip of the hot chocolate. She almost gasped with pleasure. A rush of flavours was filling her mouth; there were hints of ginger and orange, and was that liquorice? It was such a wonderfully rich taste.

'This is amazing, Dina,' she said to the assistant ladling the bubbling elixir into mugs. Dina winked. 'Nothing but the best from our kitchen.'

The unexpected treats were going down well with the guests. An eager crowd had gathered around the table which had been set up and many were coming back for seconds. Ferelith didn't understand how the kitchen staff had managed it. The order couldn't have been something they were expecting. Yet within fifteen minutes of them being contacted by her father, a silver tureen of the most delicious hot chocolate in the world had been brought outside on a trolley.

With it were wicker baskets filled with Christmassy delights; biscuits iced like Christmas trees, silvery snowflake crunches, glittery spheres full of creamy flavours.

At least the refreshments had distracted the young people. Instead of chasing each other all over Geraint's flower beds, they were becoming intoxicated by the hot chocolate.

Something caught Ferelith's eye. A flatbed lorry was making its way slowly up the hotel's driveway. On its rear was a towering potted Christmas tree tethered carefully with ropes. It came to a stop outside the front entrance and Geraint climbed out of the driver's cab. He gazed at the scene around him, the grounds of the hotel all covered in white, as if stunned. Ferelith's heart sank; she couldn't imagine what he was thinking.

He stooped to pick up a handful of the artificial snow as she hurried over.

'I'm so sorry about this, Geraint. They arrived after you'd gone; three men in a huge lorry. They sprayed the artificial snow everywhere and left. I couldn't believe how quickly they did the job.'

He tipped his hand and let the artificial snow drift back down to the ground apart from one piece. He unrolled the thin strip of paper.

'It's meant to be biodegradable,' Ferelith said hesitantly.

He gave a rueful snort.

'I wonder if the worms realise that.'

Ferelith spotted Holly and Bree with a group of friends. They had gathered some of the artificial snow into a large pile and were taking turns to throw themselves onto it.

'The youngsters got a bit excited when the snow first appeared. They were running around all over the place.'

Geraint just smiled briefly. 'It's Christmas; they should be enjoying themselves. And if the grounds are covered in artificial snow then that means less work for us.'

Ferelith was grateful for his attitude, though she suspected that he couldn't feel as relaxed about the situation as he appeared.

He clapped his hands together. 'Anyway, me and the lads had better get on with swapping the Christmas trees round.'

Ferelith turned to the back of the lorry. 'That one looks a beauty.'

He nodded. 'I was lucky. It had been ordered for a special event that was cancelled at the last minute. Normally you have to order potted trees this size months ahead of time.'

'Everything is ready for you. The tree inside has been cleared of its decorations. Though it seems such a waste just to get rid of it.'

Geraint shook his head. 'I've been in touch with the local hospice. They said that they would love to have the tree to put up in their lobby. I'll take it round there later.'

'That's such a good idea; thank you, Geraint.'

'No problem.' He pressed a button on his phone and lifted it to his ear. 'Hi,

Faisal. Gather up the troops and bring them round to the front of the building. We have a couple of Christmas trees to move.'

Ferelith watched as the ground staff gathered round the tree and began untying its ropes. An artificial snowball whizzed past her nose. 'Careful,' she laughed at two youngsters racing by.

'Sorry,' they cried in unison. They disappeared round the corner of the building and Ferelith made her way into the hotel.

There was a pleasant atmosphere in the reception area. With Miss Buckley-Tone's music playing quietly in the background, guests were relaxing in the armchairs, chatting together and enjoying their morning coffees.

'We have a problem, Ferelith,' came a voice in her ear.

It was Jane Soutar, the chief housekeeper. Earlier, Ferelith had helped Jane and a couple of her staff to speedily remove the decorations from the Christmas tree. Once the replacement tree was in place, they were planning do an equally speedy redecorating job. A task like that would normally have been done at a quiet time when there were few guests around. However, Lyle Cranford seemed to be turning all the hotel's normal routines upside down.

Jane nodded to the boxes of decorations waiting in the corner. 'It's the wooden baubles you ordered; the ones with guests' names on them along with a Christmas message.'

Ferelith smiled. 'They came out well, didn't they? I'm really pleased.'

Jane grimaced. 'That's the trouble; they came out too well. They've been really popular and people have been trying to spot the ones with their names on them.'

'That's good.'

'Perhaps. But five minutes ago, I found a little huddle of youngsters going through the box of baubles. I chased them away, politely of course, but a few of the baubles are missing.'

'You think people have taken the ones

with their names on them?'

Jane nodded. 'I suspect so. It won't be easy getting them back.'

Ferelith shook her head. 'There's no need for that. We were going to give them to the guests anyway when they left. And there are plenty of other decorations to go on the tree.'

'Talking of which,' Jane murmured.

Ferelith turned. The top of the new Christmas tree was appearing through the entrance followed a few moments later by Geraint and three of his gardening staff. They were clearly having difficulty carrying the enormous pot. They set the tree upright just inside the door.

'When we lift the tree, Faisal, put this underneath it to protect the floor,' Geraint said, handing him a square of old carpet. He and two of his men took the strain and then lifted the pot as Faisal slipped the piece of carpet into place. Geraint stood up, feeling his back ruefully. 'I wouldn't want to do this every day.'

They began pulling the tree slowly across the polished floor making sure that it didn't topple over. People watched in amused curiosity and a spontaneous round of applause broke out when it reached its destination. Faisal pulled off his woolly hat and did an extravagant bow while Geraint and the other helpers adjusted the position of the tree at Jane's direction.

Removing the other tree was less of a problem. They quickly lowered it to the horizontal and, with the eager help of some young volunteers, they carried it across the lobby and out through the entrance.

Jane gazed at the new tree thoughtfully.

'This one isn't quite as big as the other. It shouldn't take too long to decorate.'

'I'll be back to help in a minute,' Ferelith said. 'I just want to make sure that everything is all right with the old tree.'

She hurried outside where Geraint and his helpers were loading the tree onto the flat-top lorry. She watched as they tied it down carefully.

'Thanks so much for this, Geraint. I can't believe we've had to go to all this trouble just because Lyle Cranford doesn't like the idea of a traditional Christmas tree.'

Geraint pulled on a rope to check that it was tight. 'It's not a problem. If that's what he wants to spend his money on . . .' But then he turned with a frown. Shouts of excitement were rising up from the guests.

Ferelith looked round and blinked. Turning carefully into the driveway was a sleigh pulled by two reindeer with giant red scarves round their necks and tinsel round their antlers. The reindeer were being led by a grizzled-looking elf and sitting in the sleigh was a man dressed as Father Christmas. As they watched, he stood up and began waving enthusiastically. The children didn't need a second invitation. They raced down the drive towards the sleigh, cheering and shouting.

'That must be the great man himself,'

Geraint murmured in amusement. 'Lyle Cranford.'

Ferelith nodded. 'I imagine so. It looks as if he quite likes being the centre of attention.'

The scene quickly became chaotic. Some children clambered onto the sleigh while others surrounded the reindeer, which the elf didn't seem too happy about. Father Christmas was laughing and trying to keep prying hands away from the large bags of presents beside him and his hat got pulled off at some point in the process.

It took a minute or two, but calm was restored with the help of the children's parents. The sleigh got going again, moving slowly on the little wheels under its runners and eventually came to a stop in the middle of the lawn. A grinning and hatless Father Christmas with his beard dangling sideways called out 'Ho — ho — ho, and a Merry Christmas to you all!'

There was a cheer from everyone gathered round.

'I'll drink to that!' someone cried out holding up a mug of hot chocolate and that generated another cheer.

'Now don't worry, children,' Father Christmas called out. 'You'll all get a chance to ride in the sleigh later thanks to my good friend, the elf.' The elf looked at him with a startled expression. 'But first . . .'

Reaching into a small golden bag by his feet, Father Christmas brought out a handful of glittery objects and tossed them into the air. He scattered another handful. Then another. One of the objects landed by Geraint's feet and he picked it up. Ferelith gasped.

'That's a Coeur D'Amour chocolate. They're hand-made. They cost a fortune.'

'What is Christmas all about?' Father Christmas cried out.

'Presents!' came the immediate response from one of the children. There was laughter from the crowd.

'And I have some wonderful presents here which you'll be getting at our

Christmas Eve party,' he said, pointing towards the bulging sacks behind him. 'There will also be a very special pre-Christmas present for each of you.'

'What's a pre-Christmas present?' Geraint muttered.

Ferelith laughed. 'I don't think we're rich enough to know.'

Father Christmas held up a hand for silence.

'But before any of that, I have another surprise.' There was eager excitement in his eyes. 'You won't believe what will soon be coming up that drive behind me.'

Ferelith looked at him uncertainly; she wasn't sure if she liked the sound of that. She caught sight of her father nearby. He was gazing back down the driveway with an expression of concern.

6

Ferelith hurried over to her father. 'Do you know anything about this, Dad?' Lionel shook his head. 'I imagine that the surprise is something extravagant and unexpected. He tends not to do things by halves.'

'Wouldn't it have been normal for him to have warned you about whatever it is beforehand?'

Lionel gave a rueful laugh. 'I don't think normal applies to Mr Cranford.'

Ferelith looked over towards the sleigh. With his curly white beard pulled down under his chin so that it was out of the way, Lyle had called over a couple of members of the hotel's staff. They collected the bags of presents from the sleigh and began carrying them into the hotel.

'Shall I go and ask him?'

'You can try,' Lionel retorted. He looked around. 'I'll have a go at

Franklyn Boscoby. Maybe he can tell us something.'

Lyle's assistant was standing by himself nearby, talking into his phone.

Ferelith made her way over to the sleigh. Lyle had climbed down and was standing beside the reindeer with children all around him.

'Of course I flew here from the North Pole on the sleigh pulled by my two brilliant friends.'

'What are they called, Uncle Lyle?' said a girl.

'Sprinkles and Cookie,' he smiled.

The elf let out a weary sigh and muttered, 'Sparkles and Brownie.'

Lyle grinned. 'That's right — Sparkles and Brownie. We dropped in on Greenland to do some duty-free shopping, skied down Mont Blanc to gather speed, did a quick whirl round the Eiffel Tower and here we are!'

Ferelith pushed her way forward.

'I'm sorry to bother you, Mr Cranford . . .'

'Mr who?' He looked at her with an

expression of exaggerated confusion. 'I'm Father Christmas! Don't you recognise me?' He held out his hands to a nearby child and they began dancing around singing *Jingle Bells*. Immediately, the other children followed their example. Ferelith was left feeling rather foolish, surrounded by merriment with only her and the grumpy elf not joining in. She had no choice but to wait until the song had come to an end before she made another attempt.

'Father Christmas, I just wanted to ask . . .'

But someone had pressed a mug of the hot chocolate into Lyle's hand. He took a sip and his eyes widened in amazement.

'This is wonderful stuff. How perfectly glorious. From now on, we shall have this for breakfast at the North Pole every day.' He held the mug out to one of the reindeer. 'Try some, Spangles.'

'No!' The elf hurriedly interposed himself. 'The reindeer have to stick to a very particular diet.'

Ferelith pressed on. 'I'm sorry to bother you, Mr Christmas, but my father who runs the Manor was wondering if you could give him a little more information about the exciting surprise that's about to happen.'

Lyle's eyebrows rose. 'But then it wouldn't be a surprise.'

'Perhaps not but it would allow him to make suitable arrangements for . . .'

Lyle just waved a hand. 'No arrangements are needed. Everything is under control.' He turned away. 'Now where did that hot chocolate delight come from? I need more!'

As he headed off to the hot chocolate trolley followed by a trail of children, Ferelith made her way back to her father.

'No luck with Mr Cranford, I'm afraid, Dad.'

Lionel sighed. 'Franklyn Boscoby was the same. He behaved as if the security of the nation depended on no one discovering what's about to happen. I don't like surprises.'

Ferelith looked around. 'Have you

seen Geraint?'

'He's gone off to the hospice with the old Christmas tree. Did you want him for something?'

Ferelith felt herself blushing. 'Not at all . . . I just . . . no.' Her father looked at her curiously, which only made the blushing more obvious. 'I'd better get back into the hotel. Jane will be wanting help with decorating the new tree.'

* * *

As always, Ferelith felt in awe at Jane's efficiency and organisation. Normally, decorating the tree would be done at a quiet time to cause the least disruption. But the reception area was buzzing with guests, chattering and laughing in groups. The atmosphere was more like that of a cheerful party rather than the Manor's normal sense of peaceful luxury.

Jane hadn't let that affect her. The tree was set up in a corner of the hall and she had roped it off with a simple barrier decorated with coloured tinsel. Even the way she had done that was elegance personified.

'Just the person,' Jane smiled as Ferelith arrived. She and Abeer, one of the housekeeping staff, had already begun the decorating. 'You're a young thing, Ferelith. How about if you go up the ladder and hang the decorations?'

Ferelith nodded. 'Sounds good to me.'

They quickly developed an efficient routine. Abeer collected the bits and pieces from the various boxes and handed them to Ferelith who positioned them according to Jane's instructions. A few people gathered to watch and soon they were giving lots of advice, all of which Jane listened to very patiently. Though Ferelith noticed that she didn't follow any of it.

The decorations bearing the guests' names were positioned quite low on the tree so the names were easy to see, and well within reach. She wondered if Jane had decided that, since some guests were going to remove their baubles anyway, she might as well make it easy for them.

It was hard to see the effect from up the ladder but, when Jane announced that it had been done to her satisfaction, Ferelith climbed down and moved the ladder out of the way. She stepped back as Abeer switched on the lights.

There were gasps from the people gathered about; the tree looked exquisite. Everyone's eyes were drawn to it. With the lights swirling around in complex patterns, it seemed as if something magical had appeared in the corner of the reception area. Applause rose up around them as Ferelith, Jane and Abeer hugged each other warmly. 'It's perfect,' Ferelith beamed.

'So beautiful,' Abeer agreed, her eyes shining.

They finished it off by arranging large empty boxes decorated with festive wrap and extravagantly tied ribbon round the bottom of the tree. Guests had already begun to take selfies with the tree in the background. But with the barrier removed and everything else tidied away, Ferelith was able to head back outside again.

She spotted Geraint standing a little aside from the crowd. 'You have to see the new Christmas tree,' she said eagerly. 'We've just finished the decorating and it looks amazing.'

'I'll have a look at it later. Faisal and I took the old one to the hospice and set it up for them. We just got back.' He smiled. 'It's all going on here.'

Lyle Cranford in his Father Christmas outfit was being taken on a tour of the grounds by the reindeer. There were a handful of children on the sleigh with him and every minute or so it would stop and the children would swap over. Ferelith could hear Lyle leading all of them in a raucous version of Rudolph *The Red Nosed Reindeer*.

Meanwhile, a large van had parked on the lawn and a group of half a dozen people were hard at work. They had set up a sizeable octagonal structure about six feet high and Ferelith could see a hose stretching to it from round the corner of the hotel.

'Are they filling it with water?' she said

in puzzlement.

Geraint nodded. 'It's an outdoor pool. That must have been what Lyle Cranford was talking about.'

Ferelith wasn't sure whether she felt disappointed or relieved.

'It's an odd sort of surprise,' she said in puzzlement. 'I can't see people wanting to swim outside at this time of year, especially when the hotel has a whole selection of indoor pools to choose from.'

Geraint shrugged. 'I'm just glad it's nothing worse. It's only lawn there; the pool shouldn't do much damage.' His eyes narrowed. 'Hopefully.'

They watched in curiosity as an odd-looking structure was brought from the back of the van. It was a curved slope which fitted to the side of the pool, leading from the ground to the top. 'Wouldn't a ladder have been simpler?' Ferelith muttered.

Then they brought out another structure which they positioned in the centre of the pool so that there would be an area there rising out of the water.

'This is weird,' Geraint murmured.

'Certainly is.'

There was a cheering sound and Ferelith turned. Father Christmas in the sleigh was slowly approaching with the children gathered around him. The elf led the sleigh close to the recently-erected pool and brought it to a stop. Lyle stood up and held out his arms.

'Are you ready?' he cried out.

There was a muted response.

'ARE YOU READY?' he cried again and this time the response was more enthusiastic.

'Ready for what?' someone shouted out.

'You're about to find out,' he grinned. He produced a phone, which seemed rather incongruous for Father Christmas, Ferelith felt and he spoke into it briefly. 'Now watch,' he cried, his eyes bright with excitement.

Ferelith couldn't help but smile. He was like a small child at a party. Whatever else happened at the Manor that Christmas, Lyle Cranford clearly intended to enjoy himself.

'Here it comes!' he suddenly shouted, pointing to the entrance of the driveway. Another van which must have been parked nearby had appeared. Ferelith watched it approaching.

'Why does it have those holes in the side?' she murmured in puzzlement.

'I'm not sure I like the look of this,' Geraint murmured.

With everything covered in white thanks to the artificial snow, it wasn't clear to the driver where the road led. Geraint gave a grimace as the van turned and drove straight over one of the flowerbeds. Ferelith felt for him. The van reversed until it was next the octagonal swimming pool. Three women jumped out.

'Let's have a countdown,' Lyle called out. 'And while we're at it, do you think we should put a few fish into the pool?'

No one seemed sure what he was referring to. However, he had already started.

'Ten . . . nine . . . eight . . .'

The slow countdown was taken up by

the gathered guests as the trio opened the van's rear doors. They pulled out a ramp and climbed inside.

'What's that noise?' Ferelith said. It seemed familiar somehow but she couldn't quite place it. 'Is it birds?'

As the chant approached zero, Lyle rang his bell for no particular reason. 'If it's Christmas and you have snow then surely . . .'

The three women appeared again from inside the van. There were squeals from the crowd.

'I don't believe it,' Ferelith gasped.

'. . . you also need penguins!' Lyle shouted, throwing his arms out wide.

As they watched, a dozen rockhopper penguins waddled cheerfully down the ramp, all squawking happily to each other. Ferelith heard a groan of anguish from her father nearby.

'This can't be happening. What on earth have I let our hotel in for?'

7

It was barely nine o'clock in the morning. Already, a tiny hammer was pounding away at Erik's forehead. That normally didn't happen until late afternoon, when the end of his shift on the reception desk was approaching and he was beginning to long for the small glass of dry sherry awaiting him.

'I didn't sleep a wink because of the racket being made by those penguins. They were screeching away outside our window all night.'

It seemed to Erik that the penguins made more of a honking than a screeching sound. However, he didn't feel it was the moment to mention that. He fixed a sympathetic smile onto his face. A guest was unhappy and it was his duty to deal with the matter.

'I am very sorry to hear that, madam. Unfortunately, the penguins have their own keepers and are outside our control.

If you remember, they were brought here by Mr Cranford himself. I believe he hoped that they would add to the Christmas spirit at the Manor.'

Along with the artificial snow which the wind was blowing all over the place; not to mention a crate of very alarming looking hi-tech water guns which had been delivered to the hotel half an hour earlier. The sight of them had prompted Kaspar from the exercise suite to utter a volley of rapid and horrified German, the meaning of which had been fairly clear, even though Erik hadn't recognised some of the more specialised words. It was about then that the tiny forehead hammer had first put in its appearance.

'I didn't feel very much of your Christmas spirit last night,' the guest retorted. 'I came here expecting to have a relaxing time. Not to be kept awake all night listening to a bunch of yacketting birds.'

'We do have a wide selection of sleep headphones available for the use of guests,' Erik suggested. 'Perhaps they would help cut down the noise.'

'There shouldn't be any noise,' the guest snapped. 'This is supposed to be a five-star hotel. The sound-proofing in your suites ought to be more effective.'

'Perhaps a change of rooms is the answer,' Erik murmured in his calming voice. His fingers flicked over the keyboard. 'As it happens, there is a room available at the rear of the hotel looking out over the sensory garden. You shouldn't be disturbed by the penguins from there.'

'When could I move?'

'Straight away, madam. I will send a member of the housekeeping staff to pack up your things and have them transferred to your new room immediately.' Erik could see that the guest wasn't completely convinced. 'And, of course, you will find one of our luxury Welcome Packs containing a selection of fruit and chocolates waiting there to make up for your inconvenience.'

She frowned. 'No drinks?'

'As well as a bottle of Fosbury Manor Pinot Noir,' Erik added smoothly. 'Would you prefer red or white?'

Her eyes looked suddenly greedy.

'I drink both.'

'Of course, madam. I shall organise it at once.' The guest moved away with a triumphant smile, clearly feeling that she had won a great victory.

Ferelith appeared from the security room behind the reception desk.

'More problems, Erik?'

He sighed. 'Nothing too serious, Miss Ferelith. Just another guest complaining about the noise.'

Ferelith smiled sympathetically.

'When you went into the hotel business all those years ago, I don't suppose you ever thought that, one day, you would be having to deal with raucous penguins.'

'That's true. Let's just hope that things go a bit more smoothly for the rest of the day.'

'The very person. I've a bone to pick with you!'

A burly man was approaching the desk and he didn't look happy. Erik recognised him as one of the hotel's neighbours.

'Mr Hussain, I hope there's not a problem?'

'There certainly is. Last night, the wind blew that artificial snow of yours all over my garden!'

Erik stifled a groan and the tiny hammer resumed its work.

* * *

Ferelith made her way out of the hotel. An eager group of guests had gathered round the penguin enclosure. Cameras were hard at work as some of the children were allowed to help with the morning feed. However, it was Geraint whom she was looking for.

She found him with a couple of his staff raking the artificial snow on the lawn.

'You shouldn't be doing that, Geraint. It's hardly your responsibility.'

But he just smiled. 'If we're going to have artificial snow covering the grounds then at least it should look effective.'

The wind the previous night had

blown the tiny paper spirals into numerous drifts and piles. Patches of the green lawn could be seen through the white, and the ground staff were doing their best to cover them up again.

'It was actually the artificial snow that I wanted to talk to you about. There has been a complaint from one of the neighbours.'

'Mr Hussain? I saw him coming up the drive earlier.' Ferelith nodded and Geraint frowned. 'He wouldn't complain unless he had reason to. We've always had a good relationship with him.'

Ferelith explained about the artificial snow ending up in his garden during the night. Geraint grimaced.

'I thought that might be an issue. The bits of paper don't stick together; they blow around much more easily than real snow. I suspect that the guys and I are going to have a lot of raking to do over the next week or so.'

'I'm sorry about that.' Ferelith sighed. 'It's not really fair that you're having to deal with the artificial snow. It's made your job a lot more difficult.'

He shrugged. 'It's not a problem. And if it makes the guests get more into the Christmas spirit, then it will be worth it. They were certainly pleased about it yesterday, especially the younger ones. And the penguins have gone down a treat.'

The two of them turned. The feeding seemed to be over but now guests were being allowed into the enclosure, a few at a time, to get up close to the penguins. Any number of selfies were being taken. Geraint laughed.

'It's different, this Christmas.'

'That's for sure,' Ferelith murmured.

'And don't worry about Mr Hussain's garden. I'll go and sort that out now while the guys finish with the raking. I'll take round one of our garden vacuums and tidy things up for him.'

Not for the first time, Ferelith was impressed by the way he didn't grumble or complain about problems; he simply dealt with them.

'Thanks, Geraint. You're a star.' But then she had a sudden thought. 'Maybe

I'll come with you. I could take round a little something to make up for their trouble. Do you know if there's a Mrs Hussain?'

* ★ ★

'These chocolates are so delicious. They're like . . . like . . . heaven in your mouth.'

Ferelith couldn't help but smile. The small boxes of Fosbury Manor chocolates were prepared for the hotel by a specialist chocolatier and were usually only available for guests to buy at an eye-watering price. But Mrs Hussain's delight in them was irresistible. Even Mr Hussain had relented enough to try a couple.

'You must have one,' Mrs Hussain said, holding the box out to her.

Ferelith shook her head. 'No, they're for you to enjoy as an apology from us. We pride ourselves on our good relationships with our neighbours. I'm just glad that we've been able to sort out this little

86

problem.'

Mrs Hussain frowned at her husband.

'I don't know why Idris made such a fuss. It was only a few bits of paper on our lawn.'

Mr Hussain's cheeks began to flush and Ferelith hurriedly interposed.

'Not at all. You were quite right to contact us, Mr Hussain. Your garden is important to you and we had no business to allow the artificial snow to drift into it. But Geraint is vacuuming it all up and he's going to erect a temporary fence to make sure no more finds its way into your garden.'

'Why have you got pretend snow all over the grounds anyway?' Mr Hussain asked gruffly. 'It seems a bit vulgar for the Manor, really.'

In a way, Ferelith agreed with him. The snow had seemed rather magical, initially, but it was getting dirty as people walked over it. And it hardly fitted with the Manor's reputation as a luxury hotel.

'It's only temporary,' she assured him.

'It will soon be gone.'

'And did I see penguins in the grounds?' His eyes suddenly narrowed. 'You haven't rented the Manor out to make a film, have you?'

Ferelith's eyes widened in shock.

'Certainly not, Mr Hussain. We wouldn't dream of such a thing. But like the snow, the penguins are there to add a bit of Christmas spirit . . .'

'What have penguins got to do with Christmas?'

'Well . . .' Ferelith had wondered herself.

'Idris, stop harassing the poor girl,' Mrs Hussain said. 'She's done a very kind thing to come round with these chocolates. She deserves thanks not endless questions.'

Mr Hussain didn't seem convinced but Ferelith welcomed the opportunity to take her leave.

'I won't bother you any longer. I'll see if Geraint needs any help and then the two of us will get out of your way. Again, my apologies on behalf of the Manor and please do let us know if any other issues cause you concern.'

Out in the garden, Geraint was vacuuming up the last of the artificial snow.

'You've done a great job,' Ferelith said.

He put down the vacuum and pulled a plastic bag from his pocket. 'I'll walk round to see if there are any last bits of paper that I missed.'

'I'll give you a hand.'

'Thanks,' he smiled.

They checked through the flowerbeds, picking up the odd piece of artificial snow here and there.

'How are they inside?' he asked.

'They're all right, I think. The chocolates went down well with Mrs Hussain.'

'Shazia is a peacemaker; it was Idris who was upset. He's very proud of his garden and rightly too. But hopefully the fencing I put up will make sure that it doesn't happen again.'

It only took them a minute or two to make their way round the garden. Idris and Shazia were watching through their sitting room window and, as Ferelith and Geraint indicated that were leaving, Shazia lifted the chocolate box and waved cheerfully.

Geraint picked up the garden vacuum and Ferelith opened the garden gate.

'Thanks for your help,' Geraint smiled.

'It's you who deserves the thanks,' Ferelith said. 'I think it's been unfair on you and your staff to have had the grounds messed about with. I'm sure that if Dad had known what was going to happen beforehand, he would have done something about it. But Lyle Cranford seems to be the sort of person who acts first and worries about the consequences later.'

Geraint just shrugged.

'When you're as rich as he is then you can have an attitude like that. Covering everything with artificial snow because it takes your fancy . . .'

'And inviting a bunch of penguins to your Christmas party.'

As they laughed together, an odd thing happened. They looked at each other just for a moment but then their eyes held. It felt so natural, as if it was something that the two of them had been doing all their lives.

A silence stretched between them. Ferelith thought that Geraint was about to say something. She felt a strange rushing sensation. But then his expression became uncertain and he seemed to change his mind. Though as he turned away, her heart continued to race.

8

The coffee lounge was filled with noise. It was a very pleasant, comfortable room. The French windows all along one wall opened out onto a patio area and, beyond that, there were the gardens at the rear of the hotel.

Most mornings, it was a peaceful place with people quietly reading their newspapers or talking in twos and threes. However, Lyle Cranford had asked for everyone to gather there for a special announcement. The lounge was chock-a-block and there was a buzz of curiosity in the air.

Ferelith stood quietly by the door. Her father had asked her to keep an eye on things in case the announcement involved anything that he needed to know. Already, they had learned that the unexpected was usually just round the corner where Lyle was concerned.

She winced slightly as she caught sight

of group of children over in one corner. They were involved in an energetic game, chasing each other over and round some sofas and armchairs. It wasn't the sort of behaviour that was normally seen at the Manor, but the current group of guests had introduced their own standards and no one seemed the slightest bothered by the racket that the children were making.

Some other youngsters, teenagers mostly, were sitting round the tables out on the patio area. Ferelith could see Holly and Bree among them. They were busy with their phones as they chattered and laughed together.

The lounge staff made their way discreetly round the room, delivering coffees and pastries and collecting empty cups and plates.

As Ferelith was watching, a cushion flew past the face of one of the waitresses and she almost dropped the tray in her hands.

'Quentin, behave!' a voice barked in irritation.

'Soz,' came the cheerful reply, though

it sounded wholly unapologetic.

There was a sudden clamour. Ferelith turned. Lyle Cranford, with Franklyn Boscoby at his side, was arriving. His face lit up with a smile and he waved in amusement with both hands at the jokey cheer which rose up.

Ferelith looked at him curiously as he walked past. One of the kitchen staff had been talking about how much he was worth. Ferelith couldn't recall the amount but it was ridiculously huge.

Yet he seemed like a completely normal person. He was in his mid-thirties, a ready grin on his face, clothes which could have come from a discount store. There was nothing about him which suggested that he was a billionaire many times over, except perhaps the close presence of Franklyn Boscoby whose eyes always seemed to have a suspicious and disapproving expression.

The two men were followed by three members of the hotel staff. They were pushing laundry trolleys filled with colourful cardboard boxes stamped with the FastChat logo.

Lyle made his way over to the far end of the lounge and, without a moment's thought, he climbed up onto a table so that he could be seen by everyone. He smiled broadly.

'Sorry to keep you waiting, folks. Firstly, a very warm welcome to you all, particularly to anyone I haven't had a chance to speak to yet. I hope you're having a great time here at Fosbury Manor. Isn't this a wonderful place?'

Applause rose up around the room along with some whistles and cheers. Ferelith felt herself smiling. The hotel's routines had been thrown out of the window since the arrival of Lyle and his guests and there had been the occasional complaint about the penguins. But it was clear that most people were having a fine time and that was the important thing.

'You may remember that, when I arrived yesterday, I promised you all a special pre-Christmas present.'

'Presents!' came an excited child's voice.

There was laughter around the room.

Lyle grinned. 'That's why I asked you to gather here this morning. It's wonderful that we can all be together this Christmas. And I don't intend to talk business in what is very much a social occasion. But in little over a month, FastChat will be launching a very exciting new product which some of you may have heard of — the GroupChat phone.' There was a rush of excitement round the room. Clearly, some of the guests had heard of it. 'The development has generated a lot of interest in the industry and we suspect that it's going to be a huge success. But no one outside the company has yet got their hands on one of the phones — until today. I am going to give each one of you a GroupChat phone to use while we're staying at Fosbury Manor.'

A volley of excitement erupted from the teenagers who had gathered inside the French windows. They began dancing about, hugging each other. A smile of amusement spread across Lyle's face at the reaction.

'What about us, Uncle Lyle?' a young boy near to him cried out. 'Do we get one too?'

'Absolutely, Jordan,' Lyle answered. 'These phones are designed for both children and adults. In fact . . .' He indicated to Franklyn Boscoby who handed him a box from one of the laundry trolleys. He handed it on to the child. 'You can be the very first to receive a Group-Chat phone.'

There was a clamour as other young people rushed forward to collect their phones. Lyle held his hands up with a laugh.

'Steady on, now; if you'll just show a little patience. We brought plenty for everyone.'

The three members of staff started pushing the laundry trolleys around the lounge and handing out the boxes. There was a mixture of responses; the youngsters tended to pull open their packages eagerly but many of the older folk reacted with little more with mild curiosity.

'While the phones are being distributed, perhaps I could tell you a little about them,' Lyle Cranford called out above the noise. 'You can use them just like normal smartphones, if you wish. However, with the GroupChat phones, there are a number of additional functions. For instance, if you switch your phone to group-mode then it becomes linked up with all the other phones in your particular group. Thanks to the integral cameras and microphones, you can see what everyone else is seeing and hear what they are hearing.'

Excited chatter rose around the room. 'Families might want to set themselves up in groups; or friends. It's your decision. I'm just curious to see what you make of the phones. This is a bit of a test-run. So use them in whatever way you wish and let me know what you think.'

There were beeps, buzzes and all kinds of other sounds rising up around the room as the phones were switched on.

'The instructions are designed to be simple to follow,' Lyle added. 'If any adults find themselves confused about what to do then I suggest that you ask a nearby youngster, that usually works.'

He was having to shout to make himself heard above the noise. 'And one last thing. A few minor problems have arisen involving the phones' batteries which our technicians are dealing with. You should be able to charge your phone yourself as normal. But if you find that there are problems then we have a multiple charger which you can use. It's capable of charging large numbers of phones at the same time.'

Franklyn Boscoby was holding up a bizarre hemispherical object. It was the size of a beach ball and looked vaguely like a robotic hedgehog.

'I'll arrange to have it situated where it can be accessed by everyone.' He held out his hands. 'Anyway, good luck with the phones. Enjoy them!'

There was sporadic applause but most people were concentrating on trying to get to grips with their phones. Already, the teenagers were back out on the patio, huddled together in an excited group all talking at once. Though Ferelith's eye had been caught by the mass of packaging which had been scattered around the lounge. That would need clearing up.

Her thoughts were interrupted by Lyle's voice. He was holding out one of the boxed-up phones.

'What about you, Ferelith? Would you like to join our testing team?'

Ferelith shook her head. 'Thank you for the offer, Mr Cranford, but I think I'll pass on that. This is a busy enough time for us as it is without having to get to grips with new technology.'

He smiled. 'No problem. But let me know if you change your mind.'

Ferelith began to help the other members of staff collect up the debris. She was amused by the different ways in which the guests were reacting to the Group-Chat phones. Some had done little more than glance at the phones and then put them to one side; they clearly weren't particularly interested in them. Others had opened up the boxes eagerly enough but were struggling to get to grips with the instructions. She cleared up around one man who was pressing button after button on his phone and muttering in annoyance that it was all too complicated and something must be wrong with the machine. However, there were guests for whom the phones were already working all too well.

'For heaven's sake, Dahlia,' Ferelith heard one woman saying urgently into her phone. 'Why did you take it to the toilet? We can see and hear everything!'

There was a shriek of horror from the phone which was suddenly cut off and Ferelith had to struggle not to burst out laughing.

She did wonder, as she went round the room with a black bag, whether she should have taken up Lyle Cranford's offer. Perhaps having one of the phones would have helped her with her work; it would have allowed the guests to contact her immediately with problems or queries.

Her eyes narrowed. Though that might have been more of a nightmare than a benefit.

Virtually all of the young people seemed to have disappeared. She wondered if that had to do with the GroupChat phones; perhaps they were already exploring the possibilities the phones had to offer. It wouldn't have surprised her if they were getting up to mischief.

Dawn, one of the other helpers, approached her. 'I think we're done, Ferelith. I'll take your bag if you want.'

Ferelith smiled. 'That's all right, I'll take the bags to the bins. I'm going outside anyway to check when the penguins are next being fed. I want to put up a notice about it on the board.'

'OK. But make sure that all the cardboard goes into the recycling hopper.'

'Will do.'

As she made her way through the lobby laden with bags, she caught sight of Erik on the front desk. He was gazing at her with an expression of horror. At

Fosbury Manor, guests didn't expect to be confronted by members of staff carrying rubbish; she should have gone out the back way.

'Sorry,' she mouthed at him in apology and turned to head for the kitchens. Three children raced past her, Group-Chat phones in hand.

'Steady on,' she laughed. She turned a corner and came upon two more youngsters, huddled over their phones.

'I can hear water,' one was saying eagerly. 'They must be at the pool!' They jumped to their feet and rushed off.

She gazed after them, shaking her head in amusement. She had no idea what game they were playing but it was clear that the young folk were taking to the GroupChat phones like ducks to water.

9

'Hi, Dandy, I'm just checking that you're still happy to act as Santa Claus at our Christmas Eve party?'

'I certainly am, Ferelith. We have an afternoon performance of the panto that day so getting to Fosbury Manor for eight o'clock won't be a problem. And the costume folk here at the theatre are sorting out an outfit for me.'

'It's going to mean a long day for you.'

She heard a rumbling laugh down the phone. 'The very generous payment I'm receiving from you will help with that. Especially if there's a wee whisky ready for me afterwards . . .'

'The best malt that Fosbury Manor has to offer will be waiting at the bar for you when you finish.'

Ferelith put the phone down. Dandy Barham was playing one of the Ugly Sisters in *Cinderella* at the local theatre. She suspected he would make a perfect

Santa Claus for the party.

She put a line through *Check Father Christmas* on her to-do list and puffed out her cheeks at the number of items still waiting to be dealt with. She got to her feet. *Check Konrad* was next.

The noise was deafening. Shrieks and squeals from the young people echoed around the pool area. Water was flying in all directions from the guns in people's hands, some of it shooting vast distances. People were clambering eagerly about the blow-up desert island in the middle of the pool and the surface of the water was in turmoil as swimmers splashed and chased each other, both adults and children.

All at once, there was a deafening sound. It was coming from the airhorn Konrad was holding up. Silence fell over the pool apart from the gentle rippling of the water. Everyone turned to him.

'Temporary truce,' he called out. 'You have two minutes to catch your breath and refill your water guns before battle recommences.'

Ferelith saw Lyle climbing out of the water.

'Blue team to me!' he shouted. 'We need to talk tactics.'

A woman on the opposite side of the pool was waving her arms.

'Quickly — red team to me. We've got them on the run!'

'Green team — fill your guns and get over here,' a third voice yelled.

Ferelith wandered over to Konrad's side.

'This looks like fun.'

He gave her a weary look. 'Fun is not the word I would choose, Ferelith. Until now, I thought that nothing in life could be as hard as preparing for the bobsleigh event at the Olympic Games.' He shook his head. 'How little I knew. This is like trying to control a mad shoal of fish in the sea.'

She grinned. 'So what's going on?'

'It is all the idea of Herr Cranford. A water battle between three teams of guests.'

'They look as if they are enjoying

themselves.'

He looked at her ruefully.

'That may be true. But I have aged ten years in the last three quarters of an hour. And there are still fifteen minutes of the chaos to go.'

'Dad asked me to check if there was anything you needed.'

He snorted. 'A dark room, something comfortable to lie on and silence,' he muttered.

She laughed. 'It will soon be over.'

'If I survive. Keep your fingers crossed for me.' He looked at his watch and lifted the air-horn.

'Are you ready?' he called out in a roar. His eyes were sparkling and Ferelith wondered if he was secretly enjoying the fun as much as those taking part.

'Ready!' voices called from round the pool.

'Then let battle commence!'

Ferelith just had time to cover her ears.

Outside, she found Geraint and his staff on the lawn with wheelbarrows full of artificial snow which they were spreading over the green patches on the ground.

'That's beginning to look like a full-time job,' she said sympathetically.

Geraint nodded. 'The trouble is that the artificial snow is starting to get grubby with people walking about on it and that's not a great look. Not to mention the wind blowing it all over the place.' He looked around. 'So we've decided to concentrate on the front of the hotel. We're collecting the snow from the sides of the building where it's mostly untouched and clean and we're spreading it here every day to try and maintain as much of a Christmassy look as we can manage.'

Ferelith smiled. 'You could always ask Franklyn to order another lorry-load of artificial snow.'

Geraint looked at her in horror. 'Don't say that. It's going to be hard enough getting rid of this lot once Lyle and his guests have gone.'

'I'm sorry about it all,' Ferelith said sympathetically. 'This can't have been what you signed up for when you took on the job.'

But Geraint just shrugged.

'It's not a problem. The grounds and gardens are here to please the guests, not me. If the artificial snow is doing that then I'm all for it.' Not for the first time, Ferelith was struck by his easy-going nature. She liked that. She was sure that, if she had been in charge of the grounds, the situation would have been driving her mad.

Geraint frowned. 'Though I'm surprised how few people are outside. It's a lovely day today.'

Ferelith told him about the events in the pool.

'It's Lyle's idea, of course. An organised battle between guests is the last thing you'd expect at the Manor but it's happening today.'

Geraint gave a quiet laugh.

'I thought I heard a racket from the exercise suite. How is Konrad coping? He's usually very strict about behaviour in the pool. It must be difficult when there's a water fight going on.'

'He's managing — just. He's insisting on all the usual rules being followed. There's no play-fighting, no running, no bombing. And people are mainly sticking to that; no one wants to get on the wrong side of a man the size of Konrad. But I got the impression that he couldn't wait to get back to dealing with our usual guests. With them, the most exciting thing that happens in the pool is people doing Jumping Jacks during aquarobics.'

'He has my sympathy.'

'But I'm keeping you from your work,' Ferelith apologised. 'I only dropped by to see if there were any problems you needed help with. Dad asked me to check round.'

Geraint shook his head. 'No, we're fine.' He smiled. 'And we have the penguins to entertain us while we work. But thank you for enquiring.'

Ferelith was just moving away when she felt the phone in her pocket vibrating. It was Lionel.

'Hi Dad, what's up?'

'Sorry to bother you, Ferelith, but some sort of problem has come up with the penguins. Angela has just been in touch.' She was one of the women who were looking after the penguins during their visit to the Manor. Ferelith heard her father give a quiet sigh. 'They're delightful creatures, of course, and they're certainly popular with the guests, especially the younger ones. But I could really could have done without the hotel being turned into a petting zoo just a few days before Christmas.'

'I'm actually outside at the moment. I'll have a word with Angela now and get back to you.'

'Thanks, love.'

As she put away her phone, she took a deep breath of the chill morning air. It was such a beautiful day; the sky was a dazzling blue. And just for a moment, as she looked around, her mind tricked her into thinking that the grounds really were covered with snow.

But her reverie was interrupted by an exasperated voice. A woman nearby was talking into her GroupChat phone.

'Semira, it's pointless to pretend you're not there. I can see you're in the games room and I can hear you and your brother giggling. We're going to visit Granny and Grandad and I want the pair of you by the front door of the hotel within the next two minutes. If I have to come and collect you myself then I promise there will be trouble.'

Ferelith smiled; it sounded as if the GroupChat phones were proving to have disadvantages as well as advantages.

She headed to the penguins. As well as having access to the pool which had been set up, the birds also had a bit of lawn and a tented enclosure where they spent their nights. The whole area was surrounded by metal barriers. She grimaced a little at the state of the lawn. In only a couple of days, the ground had become churned up and muddy. Geraint and his team would be faced with quite a challenge to restore it.

On the other hand, she couldn't help but smile at the sight of the birds hopping up the ramp and slipping effortlessly into the pool. As they swam, they avoided each other like aquatic bumper cars, clearly having the time of their lives.

Three teenage girls were standing by the enclosure. One was filming the penguins with her phone while the other two were trying to attract the penguins' attention. They called over to a woman in a blue boiler suit who was with the penguins inside the barriers.

'Please can we have a fish? We need the penguins to come over to us so that we can take a picture of them.'

The woman shook her head.

'Sorry, girls, we have to keep a very close eye on what and when the penguins eat. They're not due for another feed for a few hours yet.'

The girl doing the filming lowered her phone with a frown. 'It can't be much fun for them stuck here with nothing to do. They should be swimming in the ocean, not in some tiny pool.'

The woman smiled. 'So long as they have each other for company, a bit of space and some food to eat, they tend to be quite happy.'

The girls' GroupChat phones began to make a trilling sound all at the same time.

'It's a meeting,' one said in a low voice. 'Where?'

They glanced suspiciously at Ferelith and moved out of earshot. Ferelith smiled. Just for a moment, she wished that she was that age again.

'Hi, Angela,' she said to the woman in the boiler suit. 'My dad just got in touch with me. He said that you were having some sort of problem?'

She nodded. 'It's a small thing but it matters for the penguins. We have our feeding times twice a day when the young people can help to give the penguins their fish.'

Ferelith smiled. 'They're popular.'

'The trouble is that a few of the guests are trying to feed the penguins at other times. They throw bread and nuts to them, all kinds of things. One child kept back a couple of fish fingers from his tea and tried to give them to the penguins.'

Ferelith's eyes widened. 'Chef won't be pleased to hear that. He makes those fish fingers to a special recipe.'

'It's just that food which is suitable for humans isn't necessarily good for penguins. They have a very specific diet. If they're given other things to eat then it can harm them. There are three of us here to supervise things but we can't keep an eye on every visitor, especially at feeding time.'

'So what do you need?'

'We could do with some signs asking guests not to feed the penguins unless under supervision.'

'Of course. Tell me what you want the signs to say and I'll sort that out straight away.'

'It would also help if we had a second circle of barriers to keep the guests a little further away from the penguins. That would make it easier for us to keep things under control when feeding time is happening. Only those doing the feeding would be allowed through to the inner barrier.'

Ferelith nodded. 'I'll have a word with Geraint. I'm sure he'll be able to organise that.'

'Thanks,' Angela said with a grateful look. 'You're brilliant here at the Manor. Nothing is too much trouble.'

Ferelith gave a rueful smile. 'We're like a swan swimming. Serene on the surface but paddling away like mad creatures under the water.'

But she sighed as she headed back to the hotel. Yet more things to add to her to-do list.

10

Ferelith jogged steadily along her usual route. She had always been an early bird and she liked having a run first thing before most people were up. Quite apart from the physical exercise, which she enjoyed, it was such a lovely calm start to her morning.

It was still dark, though the sky had begun to lighten over the buildings in the distance. There was a little noise from the traffic but mostly all she had to listen to was the sound of her feet on the artificial snow. The route she had worked out around the grounds of the hotel was just under eight hundred metres. Running it six times took her around half an hour, and that was just the sort of workout she needed.

She thought about the day ahead, preparing herself. Christmas was only five days away and everything at the Manor was gathering pace. There was plenty for her to do, though none of it was too challenging, she felt.

The sudden arrival of Lyle and his party had been a shock for everyone at the hotel. The staff found themselves having to deal with very different guests from those they were used to.

However, they had all quickly adapted to the new situation. The evening before in her dad's spacious flat, Lionel had said how pleased he was at the way things had settled down.

'We may even have a fairly normal Christmas at this rate,' he had said as the two of them relaxed in front of the television with a drink. Ferelith had crossed her fingers to be on the safe side.

She breathed steadily as she ran. She didn't push herself on her morning jogs; they were just a chance to wake up her body and get her mind ready for the day.

'Morning, Ferelith,' a voice called. 'I think it's going to be another nice one.'

'Hopefully, Angela,' Ferelith called back with a wave. 'It's a beautiful sunrise.'

Angela was on her way to check the penguins. She and the other two supervisors were staying in a campervan parked at the rear of the hotel.

'Maybe I should join you on your jog tomorrow.'

'You'd be very welcome.'

Ferelith glanced at the sunrise as she ran. The colours in the sky were extraordinary; they were changing with every moment.

Her thoughts drifted towards Geraint, something which seemed to be happening more and more often. He was such a sweet person. They barely knew each other but it felt to her as if they were already friends. Though perhaps that was because he was friendly with everyone.

She would have liked to get to know him better but everything was so busy at the hotel. The Christmas rush meant no real opportunity for socialising. While she did bump into him regularly through work, it tended only to be in passing.

She pondered on possibilities as she

jogged.

'Ferelith! Ferelith!'

The voice broke into her daydreams. She came to a stop, dragging herself back to the present. But then her expression changed to one of shock. 'Angela? What's the matter?'

Angela looked distraught. She wiped her cheeks with her hands; there were tears pouring from her eyes.

'It's the penguins — they've gone!'

Moments later, Ferelith was gazing at the scene in disbelief.

'It's my own fault,' Angela cried. 'I should have set up a tent next to the penguins. It never occurred to me that they weren't safe here.'

Ferelith put an arm round her shoulders.

'You mustn't blame yourself, Angela. You and the others have been taking really good care of the penguins.'

She looked around, trying to work out what could have happened. Her immediate thought was that the penguins must have escaped somehow. But part of the fencing had been dismantled; the penguins couldn't have done that. The entrance to their enclosure was wide open; hanging from it was a scrawled banner, *Wild Meanz Free!!!*

'It must have been done by animal activists,' Angela said, looking at the banner in dismay. 'Those poor penguins; I hope they haven't come to any harm.'

Ferelith squeezed her shoulders.

'I'm sure they'll be fine. If it was protesters who did this then they'll be people who care about animal welfare. They may be misguided but I'm sure they'll take good care of the penguins.'

She quickly roused the other two supervisors and got them to look after Angela, who was very upset. Then she called her father and explained what had happened.

'They must have been freed by someone. The question is what happened to them then.'

'Might they still be somewhere in the grounds?'

'I don't think so, Dad. There was no

sign of them when I went for my jog.' A sudden thought struck her. 'Though I suppose they could be in one of the hotel buildings.'

Lionel laughed. 'I suspect that they would have been noticed.'

'I was thinking of the pool area.'

'I suppose that's possible.' He sounded doubtful. 'I'll send someone to check it out. Meanwhile, I'll contact the police and let them know. Could you have a look at the CCTV? Perhaps that will tell us what was going on.'

'Of course, Dad. I'll get right onto it.'

Having checked that Angela was all right, Ferelith headed back to the hotel. Geraint had just arrived for work. He greeted her with a smile.

'You're up and about early. Did you see the amazing sunrise?'

'It was lovely, wasn't it?' Though it seemed a long time ago now.

He frowned, noticing the worried expression on her face. 'Is everything all right?'

She explained about the disappearance

of the penguins and his eyes widened in shock.

'Somebody freed them? How was that managed without anyone hearing or seeing anything?'

Ferelith shook her head. 'I'm not sure. But I suppose if it happened in the middle of the night then there wouldn't have been anyone keeping an eye on the grounds. There's always someone on duty at the desk but they're only responsible for what's happening inside the hotel. Anyway, Dad has asked me to have a look at the CCTV. Perhaps that will give us some clues.'

'Would you like me to help? Your father asked me to liaise with the company when the system was being set up. I know how it works.'

Ferelith was surprised by the spurt of pleasure which went through her.

'What about your work?'

'Faisal and the lads can manage for an hour or so without my help.'

'Then I'd like that, Geraint. Thank you.'

★ ★ ★

Inside the hotel, there was a huddle around the reception desk. Franklyn Boscoby was speaking sharply to Lionel; he didn't sound at all happy.

'How could something like this happen without anyone noticing what was going on? It's outrageous!'

Lionel was trying to maintain a calm demeanour.

'With respect, we've done our very best at the Manor to deal with having penguins in our grounds even though we were given no warning about their appearance beforehand.'

Franklyn just brushed his words aside.

'For a hotel of your quality, Mr Cranford, I would have expected a higher standard of security.'

Lionel flushed slightly.

'The security of our guests has always been a priority. Penguins are a different matter.'

'So what do you intend to do about it?'

'The police have been informed. They're sending someone to investigate.'

'I trust they won't be using sirens,' Erik said with an expression of deep distaste. Ferelith got the impression that the very idea of police officers turning up at the Manor appalled him.

Lionel gave a rueful laugh. 'I suspect not. When I spoke to them, they seemed to find the matter rather a joke.'

'A joke?' Franklyn retorted in fury. He pulled out his phone. 'I'll going to speak to the Chief Constable. Then we'll see who's joking!'

He strode away angrily and, moments later, they heard him barking into the phone.

'Geraint and I are going to have a look at the CCTV,' Ferelith said.

Lionel nodded. 'Good. The sooner we find out what happened to the penguins, the better. I've had everywhere checked, including the pool area. They must have left the grounds, though you'd think someone would have heard something. They aren't the quietest creatures.'

A couple of youngsters had stopped nearby and were listening. 'Has something happened to the penguins?' one of them asked in shock.

Lionel smiled reassuringly. 'We're not entirely sure where they are right at the moment. But I'm sure they'll soon turn up.'

Ferelith crossed her fingers. She seemed to have been doing that a lot over the past few days.

Their inspection of the CCTV footage didn't get them anywhere. The trouble was that the cameras were situated in and around the hotel buildings. None covered the grounds themselves.

'There didn't seem to be any need for that when the system was being set up,' Geraint explained. 'The purpose of the cameras is to keep an eye out for people trying to break into the hotel. It didn't occur to anyone that we might have penguins in the grounds needing protection.'

They looked through the footage from the cameras outside the hotel buildings but there was no sign of anything suspicious. In the late evening, there were occasional glimpses of hotel guests and members of staff but their behaviour seemed perfectly normal. And later on, there was no one to be seen at all.

'I know that the penguin area is away from cameras but I thought that we would find out something,' Ferelith said in disappointment. 'Now what do we do?'

'Let's have a look at it ourselves,' Geraint suggested. 'The penguins can't have disappeared without leaving some sort of trace behind.'

Ferelith grinned. 'We should be keeping notes. They might make a TV series about this one day.'

Geraint's eyes narrowed. 'If they do, I insist on Brad Pitt playing my part.' The suggestion sent Ferelith's thoughts into a tumble. It wasn't until they were back out on the lawn that some semblance of sense returned to her mind.

'Penguins are quite messy creatures, aren't they?' she murmured. There were white squirts scattered about all over the ground.

'We can use that to follow them,' Geraint said eagerly. He pointed. 'When they left the enclosure, they must have gone in that direction.'

Ferelith had assumed that the penguins had been put into a vehicle and driven away. But it soon became clear that they had walked off themselves, presumably being herded by someone. The trail led towards the entrance to the hotel grounds. As the two of them hurried after it, Ferelith remembered her wish from earlier.

She had been hoping to spend a bit of time with Geraint and now that was happening. Though she'd had something rather more romantic in mind than following a trail of penguin poop.

They stopped when they reached the open gates at the end of the drive. The trail continued past the entrance.

'This is a bit worrying for the Manor's reputation,' Geraint said with a grin.

Ferelith frowned. 'How do you mean?'

'It looks as though the penguins have walked out on us.'

11

Ferelith looked around, trying to work out where the penguins might have gone. 'What do you think happened last night?'

Geraint frowned. 'It looks as if the birds were freed by animal activists. I can't imagine that they would have left the hotel grounds by themselves. The activists must have taken them away.'

'Would that have been an easy thing to do? The penguins are wild creatures. Wouldn't they have scattered as soon they were free from their enclosure?'

'These penguins are pretty tame. They've spent all their lives in captivity so they're used to being with humans.' He thought for a moment. 'If it was me, I would have brought along a bucket of fresh fish. Once I'd handed a few of those out, the penguins would have followed me anywhere.'

Ferelith's eyes suddenly lit up. She

had spotted a splash of white on the pavement.

'Geraint, penguin poop!'

But at that very moment, a police car turned off the road in front of them. It nosed its way through the entrance of the grounds and parked by the side of the drive. Ferelith and Geraint hurried over. A grey-haired officer climbed out of the passenger seat and straightened his uniform.

'Are you here about the penguins?' Ferelith asked him eagerly.

'We think we know the direction they went in,' Geraint added.

'Hold your horses,' the officer retorted. He gave a slow laugh. 'Or do I mean penguins? That was an odd report we received about some of them going missing. As I said to PC Lyons here, I had to check the date to make sure that it wasn't April the first.' He let out another rumbling laugh and the young constable with him smiled dutifully.

'The trail should be easy to follow,' Geraint said. 'But they were taken a while ago. We should hurry.'

The officer held up his hands. 'Steady on, now. PC Lyons is new to the force and she's still learning the trade. So let's do this by the book.' He turned to her. 'What's the first step, PC Lyons?'

The constable took out her notebook and a pen. She smiled at Ferelith and Geraint.

'Could I have your names, addresses and contact details, please?'

* * *

The next half hour or so was very frustrating. The grey-haired officer, Sergeant Banks, led PC Lyons methodically through the process of gathering all the relevant information about the incident, ensuring that she recorded it accurately in her notebook. She noted down countless names, addresses and dates of birth along with copious details about the penguins and the zoo they had come from. The two officers then took ages to minutely examine the ground around the penguin enclosure and spent even longer discussing how and why the penguins might have been released. They studied the *Wild Meanz Free!!!* banner and speculated on the material it was made from, the type of paint used, the handwriting, the spelling.

'He's more interested in getting PC Lyons to record things properly than actually finding the penguins,' Geraint muttered.

'And she writes so slowly,' Ferelith groaned. Her eyes narrowed and she looked at Geraint. 'Why don't we slip off and follow the penguins' trail ourselves?'

The two officers were studying the pool with great interest and Sergeant Banks was pointing to something in PC Lyons's notebook.

'Good idea.'They moved quietly away.

Outside the entrance to the drive, they headed for the splatter of white on the pavement that Ferelith had spotted earlier. 'There's another one up ahead,' she said, pointing. 'And another.'

Geraint snorted. 'They're not making

it exactly difficult for us to follow them.'

'The splatters are all on the pavement,' Ferelith said. 'The people who took the penguins must have been herding them, just as you suggested.'

Geraint shook his head. 'Wouldn't someone have noticed? It's not every day that you see a bunch of penguins waddling along the pavement.'

'I guess it happened in the middle of the night when there was hardly any traffic.'

'Imagine driving home after a late shift and spotting that. You'd think you were in a dream.'

'Or a nightmare!'

Their laughter was hurriedly brought to a halt. Two police cars were rushing past, their lights flashing. Ferelith and Geraint's eyes met. A hundred yards or so up ahead, the cars slowed and turned off the road.

'They've gone into the park,' Geraint said.

Ferelith's eyes widened. 'Do you think . . .'

All at once, they were both running.

Lonsdale Green was a spacious park full of walks, flower beds, bushes and trees. When Ferelith and Geraint reached the entrance, they could see the two police cars parked in the distance, their lights still flashing.

'They're by the pond,' Ferelith gasped, thinking that she wasn't nearly as fit as she had thought.

'It's got to be the penguins,' Geraint answered as they ran on.

The pond at the centre of the park was a popular picnic spot and it made for a delightful pastoral scene. There were always countless ducks, coots and geese paddling about in it, along with the occasional visiting swan. But the people gathered there in amazement that morning had never seen anything like it. Jumping in and out of the pond and splashing around in the water were a dozen rockhopper penguins.

'Stand back, everyone,' one of the police officers said. 'We're just trying to work out where these penguins might have come from.'

Ferelith made her way forward. 'I think I can help you with that, officer.'

It took a while for Ferelith to explain the situation. But while she was doing that, Geraint was on his phone to Angela back at the Manor. Within minutes, she and the other two supervisors had arrived armed with supplies of fresh fish. They were soon gathering up the penguins.

'It's been decided to take them back to the zoo,' Angela explained to Ferelith and Geraint. 'Transport is on its way. They've had more than enough excitement over the past few days. It's time they got back to their normal routine.'

'That's understandable.' Ferelith nodded. She noticed a look of relief cross Geraint's face.

One of the other supervisors was keeping the penguins calm by handing out small fish from a bag. Ferelith turned to Angela.

'Where do you keep your supplies of fish for the penguins?'

Angela frowned. 'We have a fridge for

them in our campervan. Why?'

'Geraint and I were thinking that the people who freed the penguins might have used fresh fish to lead them away.'

Angela nodded slowly. 'That makes sense. I suppose they would have brought fish with them.'

'You're probably right,' Ferelith murmured. She wandered off and keyed a number into her phone. A couple of minutes later, she hurried back to Geraint.

'I've just learned something very interesting. Last night, two dozen trout disappeared from a fridge in the hotel kitchen.'

He gazed at her in shock.

'Hang on. But that means . . .'

Ferelith nodded. 'The penguins may have been freed by people from the hotel.'

The van to collect the penguins and return them to the zoo arrived shortly afterwards. Having said warm goodbyes to Angela and her colleagues, Ferelith and Geraint hurried back to the hotel. A few things were starting to click into place in Ferelith's mind.

'Do you remember when we looked through the CCTV images from last night? There was no footage from one of the cameras at the rear of the hotel.'

Geraint nodded. 'I checked it. The camera was working perfectly but a plastic bag had blown over it. The wind, presumably.'

'Or was it put there deliberately? That camera covers one of the hotel's back doors.'

Geraint frowned. 'So if anyone had left the hotel through that door during the night, then the CCTV cameras wouldn't have shown it.'

'That's right.' She nibbled on her lower lip. 'I wonder if there's some other way of finding out if anyone left the hotel via that door.' She gave a gasp and grabbed Geraint's arm. 'I've got it. The Group-Chat phones!'

* * *

In the end, the whole story came out in a rush. Back at the hotel, they found Lyle enjoying a leisurely breakfast. Ferelith explained what they had been up to and asked if there was any way of identifying the whereabouts of the GroupChat phones.

He popped a grape into his mouth and nodded.

'The phones are fitted with trackers. They can be switched off if the users wish but I suspect that most of them are still switched on.'

'Can the trackers tell if any of the phones were out in the hotel grounds during the night?'

He frowned. 'Why do you ask?' His eyes widened in sudden realisation. 'You think guests from the hotel may have freed the penguins?'

'That's an outrageous suggestion,' Franklyn Boscoby snapped. He had been sitting at the table listening.

But Lyle himself was grinning. 'Is it, though? I wonder . . .' He took out his GroupChat phone and began pressing buttons. He laid the phone on the table so that they could all see the screen which showed a map of the hotel's grounds. 'With a bit of luck, this will give the whereabouts of the phones during the night.'

Flashing lines started appearing on the screen. Most were concentrated in a small area in the centre, which Lyle explained was the hotel itself. But as they watched, a few lines moved out into the hotel grounds.

'They're gathering at the penguin enclosure!' Ferelith gasped. 'Can you identify whose phones they are?'

Lyle nodded. 'I certainly can.'

The phones belonged to nine of the guests, all teenagers. Lyle gathered them with their parents in the coffee lounge. Nothing had been said about why they were there but the teenagers were looking rather uncertain.

Lyle organised refreshments for everyone.

'I want to start by saying that I'm not at all upset about what happened with the penguins. However, they were freed last night and I believe that those responsible are here in this room.'

There was a moment of stunned silence with the parents looking shocked and the teenagers guilty. Everyone started talking at once. The parents demanded explanations from Lyle, then from their children and the teenagers announced that they had done the right thing and that wild creatures like penguins shouldn't be kept in zoos anyway. It took Lyle some time to quieten everyone and regain the teenagers' attention.

'Believe me when I say that I don't object to what you did. You were acting out of conscience, which is a good thing, and the penguins came to no harm. In fact, it was probably a bit of an adventure for them. So, as it happens, I admire you for your actions.' The parents didn't look so convinced. 'I'm also delighted that you were using your GroupChat phones to help you.'

'Was it because of the phones that we were caught?' one of them asked suspiciously.

Lyle smiled. 'It was, I'm afraid.' The

teenagers all began to protest angrily and Lyle had to raise his voice to make himself heard. 'But if you'll listen, I can show you how to switch off the trackers on your phones. So we'll have both learned something from the experience.'

Ferelith and Geraint wandered outside.

'It's a whole different life for them, isn't it?' Ferelith murmured.

'I'm just glad that we found out what happened.' Geraint grinned. 'And don't tell anyone but I'm quite glad we've got rid of the penguins as well.'

To their surprise, they found Sergeant Banks and PC Lyons still at the enclosure.

'But the penguins have been found,' Ferelith said. 'They should be well on their way back to the zoo by now.'

Sergeant Banks gave her a lofty look.

'That may be so but there is paperwork still to be completed.' He turned back to his colleague. 'Now, PC Lyons, let's go through your notes one last time to make sure that you haven't missed any details.'

Ferelith turned away with Geraint, a baffled expression on her face.

'Do you ever get the feeling that everyone in the world is a little bit mad? Apart from us, of course.'

12

'I don't see what the problem is. You have a celebrity staying at your hotel. Lyle Cranford is news wherever he goes. It will make a great story for my paper's readers.'

Erik raised himself to his full height. 'I can assure you that guests at Fosbury Manor haven't the slightest interest in appearing in newspaper stories.'

'It will mean free publicity for the hotel.'

Erik's expression became one of icy disdain.

'Neither is the Manor interested in free publicity. It advertises itself by reputation alone.'

The woman looked at him thoughtfully.

'I think I'd like to talk to someone more senior.'

Erik wasn't impressed. 'I'm afraid that the hotel manager is much too busy.'

The woman tried to speak but Erik

immediately held up a hand to silence her.

'I shall inform him of your request. If he wishes to talk to you then he will get in touch.'

The corners of her mouth twitched in amusement. 'Please yourself.' She held out a card. 'Here are my contact details. Sometime in the next hour would be helpful. I'd like to do the story for tomorrow's issue.'

Erik took the card with the very tips of his fingers. 'I shall pass the information on.'

Ferelith couldn't help but smile. She had been sitting at the front desk doing some admin when the woman had appeared. Layanna Parker worked on one of the tabloids and had somehow learned about the story of the escaping penguins and the link with Lyle Cranford. She had turned up at the hotel seeking more details, but had been faced with a brick wall in the shape of Erik.

Layanna gazed round the reception area.

'I could have a word with some of your

guests while I'm waiting to hear back from the manager.'

Erik's eyes flashed. 'You will NOT speak to any of our guests,' he said in an icy voice.

'Then perhaps one or two members of your staff?' Layanna's eyes drifted over to Ferelith who quickly looked away; she had no wish to get involved. But Layanna's eyes had suddenly narrowed. She moved across the desk to where Ferelith was sitting.

'We were sent photos of the penguins in the park. Weren't you in some of them?'

Erik hurriedly interposed.

'Neither will you speak to members of our staff. Now I must ask you to leave, Ms Parker. We are very busy and I believe that your business with us is over.'

She looked at him for a moment, then at Ferelith. Ferelith got the impression that she wasn't intimidated in the slightest by Erik and was simply deciding on her next step. She switched on a beaming smile.

'Of course. I shall leave you to your very important work. Thank you for your time.'

She turned and moved off across the reception hall, the elegant curves of her swaying hips drawing a number of eyes. Ferelith shook her head in amusement.

'Could I ask a favour, Miss Ferelith?' Erik murmured.

'Of course, Erik.'

'Could you check that she actually does leave the grounds?'

Ferelith rose to her feet. 'OK, I'm on my way.'

Standing on the steps outside the hotel, she watched the journalist striding off down the drive. Despite Erik's suspicions, there was no sign of Layanna lingering. Hurrying past the entrance to the driveway, she stopped on the pavement. She took out her phone and pressed it to her ear, gazing back at the hotel. Ferelith watched her thoughtfully. It didn't look as though Layanna had forgotten about the story.

However, the matter was quickly driven out of her mind. There were only four days until Christmas and the hotel was gearing up in preparation for their renowned celebrations. With such different guests, the staff were having to cope with a whole range of unexpected issues. However, they were pulling together and many guests had spoken appreciatively of the relaxed, happy atmosphere throughout the Manor.

Ferelith felt she was in a constant rush as she dealt with one matter after another. As soon as she sorted out the items at the top of her To-do list, more things were added to the bottom. The staff were all under pressure and it was a godsend to have someone like her available to deal with unexpected problems. But though her days were breathless and non-stop, they were exciting. It was like being on a roller-coaster; she was never sure what was round the corner.

★ ★ ★

That afternoon, a message reached her from Geraint. He wondered if he could have a word when she had a moment. She didn't exactly drop everything and run — staff at the Manor were far too dignified to run anywhere. But she was on her way out of the hotel within twenty seconds of the message getting to her. There was something about him which drew her like an elastic band.

Geraint was standing with Faisal on the front lawn.

'Goodness, you've been busy,' Ferelith said, gazing about in admiration.

Dozens of shrubs in pots had been arranged to make a large circle. Their leaves were a dramatic mixture of Christmas colours and the pots had all been decorated with tinsel.

'I had a brainstorming session with the ground staff this morning,' Geraint said. 'This is the part of the lawn where the penguins were based. It's in a real mess at the moment and we need to keep people off it so that the grass gets a chance to recover. But we decided that it would be a bit boring just to put up some sort of barrier.'

'So what's this?'

He smiled and held out his hands. 'You are looking at the Fosbury Manor Christmas Wishing Well!'

Ferelith's eyes widened. 'I see.' Though she didn't really. 'Why are there lots of hoops on the ground inside the circle?'

Eagerly, he began to explain.

'Imagine you're a guest at the hotel and you have a secret Christmas wish of some sort. That wish is going to be tossed into our wishing well.'

'Oh — kay,' Ferelith said uncertainly.

'Next to each of the hoops there will be a sign explaining what happens to any wishes which land inside it. They'll say things like *Your wish will come true!* or *Santa knows what you want!* or *Bad luck* — try again!'

Ferelith frowned as she tried to understand.

'So people write wishes on pieces of paper?'

'We could provide some in star shapes.'

Ferelith nodded slowly. 'That would work. And we could supply glitter pens so the wishes could be decorated. Then what? They just throw the wishes in?'

'That's where we had our best idea. We're going to use a leaf blower.' There was one by his feet and he picked it up. 'Do you have a small piece of paper?' Ferelith searched in her pockets and brought out an old receipt. 'Fold it up,' Geraint said and switched on the blower. 'Now throw it up,' he called. She did so and, blasted by the leaf blower, the receipt flew high into the air, then drifted down to land in one of the hoops.

'We thought we could run two or three sessions a day where people could have their Christmas wishes blown into the wishing well.'

'That sounds like a great idea,' Ferelith said. 'I think the younger guests especially will love it.'

'It's just a bit of fun, but the point is that it will keep people off the churned-up ground.'

'So is there something you want my

help with?'

'We need some signs. One to explain what the wishing well is all about and others to go with each of the hoops. Then there are the star-shaped pieces of paper. And the pens, of course.'

Ferelith could feel her to-do list growing by the moment. She smiled ruefully.

'No problem, leave that to me.'

'Brilliant.' Geraint beamed. Unexpectedly, he stepped forward and took her in a hug. Ferelith felt herself beaming too; who cared about to-do lists? He stood with his arms around her and it occurred to Ferelith that, if she didn't move, he might forget to let her go.

But a voice suddenly broke into her thoughts.

'Excuse me, there's someone hiding in the bushes and taking photographs of people.'

She felt Geraint's shock as he let go of her. Two young guests were gazing at them.

'Taking photographs?' Ferelith echoed. One of the girls nodded. 'He's in those bushes by the entrance of the hotel. We spotted him when we were playing hide-and-seek.'

★　★　★

'He got away, unfortunately,' Ferelith said. 'I think he realised that he'd been spotted.'

Lionel was gazing at her with concern. 'Did you get a good look at him?'

Ferelith shook her head. 'Not really. But he had two cameras with him; one slung round his neck and the other in his hand. Both with long lenses.'

'Paparazzi,' Franklyn said in disgust. 'They're like parasites.'

Lyle just shrugged. 'They have their job to do.'

When Ferelith had informed her father about the photographer, he had immediately contacted Lyle and Franklyn. Ferelith explained what had happened and Lionel told them about the visit earlier to the hotel by Layanna Parker.

'The two things must be connected,'

Franklyn said, looking angrily at Lionel. 'What's going on at this hotel? The security is far too lax. First it was the penguins being removed from the grounds without anyone even knowing. And now this.'

Ferelith felt a spurt of irritation at his words. She didn't like the idea of the hotel being blamed. It was surely because of Lyle that all these things were happening?

But Lionel was looking troubled.

'The security of our guests is an absolute priority at the Manor. And I would argue that there's no problem at all with the hotel itself.' He frowned. 'Though perhaps there is a problem with the grounds.'

'So what do you intend to do?' Franklyn demanded.

Lyle suddenly leaned forward, his eyes bright with enthusiasm.

'I know what the answer is — motion detectors!'

13

Ferelith's phone began to chirrup. She picked it up with a mutter of frustration. She knew what the call would be about. 'Don't tell me, Erik. The motion detectors have picked up another signal?'

'You've guessed it, Miss Ferelith. Down by the sensory garden. Would you be good enough to check it out?'

'Of course, I'll go now.'

She looked at her computer screen with a weary sigh. All morning, she had been trying to finish the signs for Geraint's wishing well but she was constantly being interrupted by requests from Erik to check out alarms from the motion detectors. They came through to the front desk and he passed them straight on to her.

Lyle had been so enthusiastic.

'It's a new system we've been developing at GroupChat. The detectors constantly sample visual information from a particular area and detect any changes that occur. If the degree of change reaches a significant level then an alarm signal is automatically triggered.'

As he had told them in a torrent of detail about how the detectors worked, Ferelith had quickly got lost. She suspected her father had been the same but there was no holding Lyle back. He described how he would arrange to have detectors installed around the grounds that very afternoon, sounding full of excitement. He was clearly a person in love with technology.

She saved her work on the computer and got to her feet. It was time to visit the sensory garden.

'The trouble is that there's been a breeze today,' Geraint said. 'Every time the wind picks up, the artificial snow starts blowing about. For the detectors, it seems as if the whole world has begun to move so it sends off an alarm signal.'

'It's turning out to be a real pain for me,' Ferelith muttered.

'I was chatting to the woman who

came to install the detectors yesterday. She said they're actually very stupid. They can't tell the difference between a hoodlum creeping about and some particularly active sparrows. Motion detectors work fine inside buildings at night where everything is still. But out here in the real world, things are moving all the time.'

'Anyway, there's nothing unusual happening here; it's just another false alarm.' Ferelith sighed. She looked around. 'Though this is a really pretty place. You and your staff have done great work here.'

Geraint smiled, clearly pleased. 'We've gone to a lot of effort to create a garden that engages all the senses. It's somewhere peaceful to spend a bit of time. I could show you around if you want.'

Ferelith felt her heart speed up. There was something about the way he had made the suggestion, as if it was more than a casual invitation.

'I'd like that,' she said, trying to ignore the flush rising in her cheeks.

'What about this evening? You'll get the benefit of our night-scented plants. They're amazing.'

She nodded. 'OK, Geraint. I look forward to it.'

As she made her way back to the hotel, she decided that visiting the sensory garden definitely counted as a first date between them.

'I'm going on a date ... I'm going on a date,' she sang to herself and did a little skip. But then her phone sounded. It was Erik.

'I've checked out the sensory garden, Erik. Nothing unusual is going on there.'

'Thank you for that, Miss Ferelith, but I'm afraid I've had another alarm — from the lily pond.'

She let out an anguished groan. 'This is ridiculous! I'm going to speak to my father.'

★ ★ ★

'But this isn't something to be disappointed about. The fact that the motion detectors aren't working perfectly is actually a good thing!' When Ferelith had told her father about the disruption caused by the false alarms, Lionel had contacted Lyle and Franklyn. However, Lyle didn't seem put out in the slightest. 'This always happens with new technologies. Because they've never been used before, no one is sure how to make the most of them. So you try them out and learn from your mistakes.' Lyle held his hands out with a wide smile. 'It's all a bit of an experiment really.'

Ferelith had caught sight of her father's face. He managed a luxury hotel with an international reputation; he clearly didn't like the idea of the Manor being used as a science lab to try out the latest technologies from Lyle's company.

'There's just too much movement in the grounds for the detectors to cope with,' Ferelith explained. 'They're setting off an alarm every couple of minutes.'

Lyle nodded. 'You're right. The technology isn't appropriate to the situation.' He turned to Franklyn. 'You'd better arrange to have the detectors switched off and removed.'

'I'll see to it straight away,' Franklyn said. 'But we're still left with the problem of security. There's nothing to stop journalists, paparazzi or whoever just wandering into the hotel's grounds with no one knowing who they are or why they're there. In my opinion, the hotel's CCTV coverage should be expanded to cover the grounds.'

Lyle grimaced. 'I'm not sure that's the most effective solution. You'd need a lot of different cameras as well as someone to keep an eye on all the footage they collected.'

Ferelith's eyes narrowed; she had an idea who that would be. But Lyle was shaking his head.

'No, we need something different.'

'What do you have in mind?'

Lyle pondered for a moment. Suddenly his eyes lit up. He looked round at them eagerly.

'I have the perfect solution. What we need is an infra-red security system!'

★ ★ ★

Geraint laughed in disbelief. 'You're joking? The movement detectors are being removed after less than twenty-four hours?'

Ferelith nodded.

'Lyle Cranford doesn't hang about. The infra-red system is already being installed in their place.'

Geraint nodded towards some men working on the roof of the hotel.

'I suppose that's what those guys are up to?'

'According to Lyle, they're setting up an array of infra-red cameras which will detect heat sources within the grounds. Apparently, the plan is to adjust the cameras' sensitivity so they won't pick up small animals or birds. However, any people in the grounds will be shown. They'll just be a yellow and red outline. But the system will detect people hiding in bushes or whatever.'

'So will you be responsible for checking out the images and identifying anyone who shouldn't be in the grounds?'

'I've no time for that,' Ferelith retorted. 'I need to get on with the wishing well signs, for a start. All I need is a bit of time without distraction.'

'That's good. It's already attracting interest and I'd like to get it up and running. So who will be responsible for checking the infra-red images?'

'That's the thing that has got Lyle so excited. He's setting it up so that the images can be accessed by anyone with a GroupChat phone. If the guests have any suspicions, they can do the checking themselves.' She grinned. 'He says the system should be handy for children playing hide-and-seek in the grounds.'

Geraint shook his head. 'It all sounds mad to me. But I'd better get on with my work.' He looked at Ferelith. 'Are you still on for our visit to the night-scented garden?'

'I am. And I'm really looking forward to it.'

* * *

It wasn't really like a date at all, Ferelith decided. When two people went on a date, they focussed on each other; at least that was the idea. But all Geraint could think about was his sensory garden. He was so enthusiastic about it.

He told her that he'd got the idea from a visit to the Chelsea Flower Show a couple of years before when he'd been awestruck by something very similar. It had made him determined to create his own version back at the Manor.

'When people choose flowers for their gardens, they usually concentrate on how the plants look and smell. That's understandable, of course. But we have three other senses as well and the purpose of this garden is to engage them all.'

Once he got talking, Ferelith didn't even attempt to interrupt; it would have been like trying to hold back a waterfall. There was something so sweet about his eagerness. It was as if he had a precious treasure which he longed to share.

'Close your eyes and feel the bark of this tree.' Ferelith felt him lead her hand gently. 'Isn't it wonderful? And these leaves — aren't they extraordinary? They almost feel like fur.'

Her hand seemed so at home in his. When he let her go, she felt a little sag of disappointment. Night had fallen but there were solar-powered lights here and there along the paths. There was enough light for them to see each other.

'Now close your eyes again and just listen.' Silence fell but she could sense him next to her; it was a strangely intimate moment. Then her ears attuned to the sounds.

'. . . the trickling of the water from the little fountain... how peaceful is that . . . the whisper of the leaves as if they're talking to each other . . . can you hear the rustling? . . . that'll be a hedge-hog . . .'

It may not have been a proper date but, for Ferelith, it still seemed as if there was magic in the air. The scents were the best thing of all.

'Smell this honeysuckle,' Geraint murmured. 'And this viburnum. What about this skimmia?'

The names meant nothing to her but as their heads came together to smell the extraordinary perfumes, her mind began to swirl and fly. She had no doubt that Geraint was only thinking of the plants. But his presence next to her in the darkness with all her senses afire made her feel as if they had slipped into a wonderful dream.

* * *

'Hello, girls, are you having a nice evening?'

Holly and Bree were sitting shoulder-to-shoulder on the steps outside the front of the hotel. They were huddled together over Holly's GroupChat phone and, when they looked up and saw Ferelith and Geraint, their eyes widened.

'Not as nice as your evening,' Holly retorted and the two girls burst out laughing.

Ferelith smiled uncertainly. 'We've just been to the sensory garden.'

'We know!' they retorted in unison.

'The scents of some of the flowers are amazing.'

'It should be called the Garden of Luuurrvve,' Bree said and their laughter redoubled.

Ferelith looked at them in puzzlement.

'Am I missing something, girls?'

Holly turned her phone so that Ferelith could see the screen. 'We've been looking at the map from the infra-red cameras to see if there was anything going on in the grounds.'

Bree cackled. 'There was one real hotspot!'

'I'm not quite with you,' Ferelith said, though she was starting to get a sense of what they might be talking about. She sat down beside them. On the screen of Holly's phone was an outline map of the grounds, lit up in a fluorescent green with patches of yellow here and there.

'Those patches are people,' Holly said. 'You can see the three of us together and Geraint standing a little way apart.'

The patches were only rough outlines

of human shapes but they were clear enough. Holly fiddled with the controls of the screen and the map changed. 'This is the sensory garden.' She fiddled around some more. 'And this was it five minutes ago.' She increased the image so that two people could be clearly seen at the centre. 'That's you and Geraint.' Holly nudged Bree and the two of them giggled. 'Having a lovely time.'

Ferelith gazed at the screen. It was occurring to her that the images they were looking at were available to everyone with a GroupChat phone.

'But Geraint and I were just smelling the flowers together.'

'Of course you were!' Holly cackled. The two girls fell back, hooting with laughter and waving the screen which showed Ferelith and Geraint with their heads together as if kissing passionately.

14

'I don't want another level of security at the Manor,' Lionel protested. 'There's no need.'

'But this would be so simple to establish,' Lyle said eagerly. 'Everything is already set up on the GroupChat phones. All that's required is for it to be connected to the security cameras.'

Ferelith was saying nothing. She had been keeping her head down all morning. No one had actually mentioned her visit to the sensory garden with Geraint the night before. However, she had noticed some amused glances and sidelong looks from one or two of her colleagues.

It wasn't that she had anything to feel ashamed about. On the contrary. But when she thought about it — and she seemed to be thinking about it almost continuously — she felt that she wouldn't have been entirely unhappy if Geraint had tried out a kiss or two with her in the garden. But he hadn't, and it was very frustrating to think that others suspected that they had.

However, the last thing she wanted was for the subject to be brought up with her father. So she had been sitting quietly in Lionel's office getting her instructions for the day when Lyle appeared, full of enthusiasm. He'd had a new idea.

'Facial recognition,' he had said without a word of greeting. 'I don't know why I didn't think of it before. It's there on the GroupChat phones as standard. This is the perfect opportunity to try it out.'

Of course, Lionel could have expressed outrage. He was the manager of the hotel; it was his office. Lyle had no business bursting in without warning. For all he knew, Lionel and Ferelith might have been discussing a matter of life and death. As it happened, they had been talking about the laundry rota but that was neither here nor there.

On the other hand, Lyle was a billionaire many times over. And for some reason that made it hard to stand up to him. So Lionel and Ferelith listened as he explained his latest brilliant plan.

According to Lyle, linking the phones' facial recognition software to the hotel's security system would be an easy matter. Then people who were picked up by the Manor's CCTV cameras would be automatically identified.

'If the system finds someone who isn't either a guest at the hotel, a member of staff or an approved visitor then an alert will be raised and that person can be checked out,' Lyle said. 'It's all very simple. Foolproof, really.'

Ferelith wasn't convinced. 'You said that about the motion detectors and I ended up having to check out dozens of false alarms which were just caused by the artificial snow blowing about.'

Lyle waved a hand dismissively.

'That was a case of the right technology being used in the wrong situation. This is very different.' He looked at Lionel. 'So what do you say? Shall we install the facial recognition software?'

Lionel grimaced. 'I can see that there might be some advantages but . . .'

'Excellent.' Lyle jumped to his feet. 'I'll go and set things up now. You won't regret it!'

The silence in Lionel's office was like the calm after the rush of a storm. He shook his head.

'I don't know what it is about that man. He's like a force of nature. I find him impossible to resist.'

'He's certainly enthusiastic about his technology.'

Lionel frowned. 'Talking of which, someone earlier made an odd reference to the infra-red cameras. It was to do with you and Geraint and the sensory garden. Do you have any idea . . .'

Ferelith hurriedly sat up. 'None at all, Dad. Anyway, about the laundry rota . . .'

As she left Lionel's office, she resolved to spend the day cracking on with all the items on her to-do list and to keep well away from any gossip.

She couldn't work out whether she wanted to see Geraint or not. She wasn't sure what he thought of the silly rumours about what had happened between the two of them in the sensory garden. It had felt awkward the night before when Holly and Bree were laughing about the whole thing. But neither she nor Geraint had mentioned it when they parted afterwards. Now she didn't know what she ought to say when they did get together. The whole thing was a mess.

She had adopted the little security room behind reception as her office and, as she made her way there, she felt rather grumpy. It was all Lyle Cranford's fault, him and his experimental technologies. So she wasn't best pleased to find him there when she arrived. He was tapping away rapidly at the keyboard of the computer which controlled the security system.

His face lit up. 'Ferelith, the very person. I've got everything set up here. Let me show you how it works.'

What she wanted was tell Lyle that she had a to-do list as long as her arm and no time to waste on being shown how complicated things worked. But instead, without quite knowing how it had happened, she found herself sitting next to him while he demonstrated the new system.

'The software is linked into facial recognition data banks all around the world,' he said eagerly. 'Because I'm a well-known figure, I'll automatically be recognised. But the guests and staff at the hotel will have to be logged on as approved people and that will be your job.'

Ferelith blinked. 'My job? Hang on a minute. I already have . . .'

There was a ping from the computer and Lyle let out a whoop. 'Here we go. The system has identified its first unknown face.'

Ferelith frowned. 'But that's Erik on the front desk.' She didn't think that he would be best pleased by the image either. He had been caught in mid-sentence and there was a very odd expression on his face, as if he had just swallowed a bee.

'Of course it is,' Lyle smiled. 'So you

type Erik's name into that box there and click on 'Approved'.' Ferelith did as he had instructed. Lyle smiled. 'Simple. Now, whenever the system sees Erik, it will recognise him.' There was another ping. 'What about that person?'

'It's Gabrielle, the barista.'

Lyle smiled. 'You know what to do.'

'Yes, but . . .'

But Lyle was getting to his feet. 'Excellent. The system is up and running.' He rubbed his hands together. 'Now for some breakfast. Your kitchen does the most amazing scrambled eggs. I'm becoming obsessed with them. Bye, Ferelith. And thanks!'

She looked slack-jawed at his disappearing back. There were so many things that she wanted to say, most of them involving her telling him that already had more than enough on her plate. But it was too late; he was gone.

The computer pinged at her and then again. She gazed at the screen with a sour expression.

Ferelith was soon hard at work putting

names to the different faces identified by the system. However, she quickly came upon a problem. While she knew the names of the members of staff, it was a different matter when it came to the guests. She recognised most of their faces but, for many of them, she had little idea of their names. And the computer was now pinging at her regularly, demanding to have them identified.

She got to her feet in frustration. It was no good; Lyle would have to find someone else to do the job. But as she appeared in the reception area, Holly and Bree spotted her and raced over.

'Hi Ferelith,' Bree said eagerly. 'Did you sleep well last night?'

Holly grinned. 'Did you dream all night about the lovely Geraint?' She clutched her heart. 'Oh Geraint, how I love you,' she sighed plaintively.

'Enough, girls,' Ferelith said, giving them one of her looks. But then an idea came to her. 'Are you doing anything at the moment?'

Holly looked at her suspiciously.

'Why?'

'There's something you could help me with.'

The two girls took to the work with great enthusiasm. They were fascinated by the idea of the facial recognition system, especially when they learned that it was on their GroupChat phones. They bombarded Ferelith with questions which she was mostly unable to answer. But they did help with identifying the guests.

'That's Auntie Cath with Uncle Stewart . . . look at Rodney's face; he looks like a squirrel . . . that's my Nana, I'm not sure what her real name is . . .'

The girls were full of fun and Ferelith found she was enjoying herself. They'd even stopped teasing her about Geraint when Holly had a thought.

'Let's see how good the system is at identifying us, Bree,' she said eagerly. She lifted her phone. 'Make a face.' Bree twisted her face into a hideous grimace and Holly took a photo. She knew how to upload the image onto the facial recognition system and, within seconds, it had been approved. The girls fell about laughing.

'It recognised you even though you looked like a gargoyle!' Holly hooted. They tried to outwit the system by pulling the most horrible expressions but their faces were recognised each time.

Then all at once Holly gripped Bree's arm. 'I've just had a brilliant idea.'

'What's that?' Bree asked.

Holly glanced at Ferelith and the corners of her mouth twitched in amusement. There was a wild look in her eyes as she jumped to her feet.

'Come on, I'll tell you outside.'

'Hang on a minute, girls,' Ferelith called. 'What are you up to?'

But it was too late. They were gone.

In fact, most of the guests had been identified by then. The computer only made the occasional ping and Ferelith was able to get on with her to-do list. She was designing labels for the presents which Father Christmas would be handing out to guests at the Christmas Eve party. It was vital that no one was missed and she was deep in concentration when the computer surprised her with a different sound, a sort of dong. She glanced at the screen. The facial recognition system had recognised a face but this time it was someone who wasn't supposed to be at the Manor. Ferelith gazed at the image in shock. She got to her feet and poked her head round the door.

'Erik, is George Clooney staying at the hotel?'

His left eyebrow lifted visibly.

'Not that I'm aware of, Miss Ferelith. Why?'

'Because according to the new system, he's in the games room at the moment.'

The computer donged again and Ferelith hurried back to it to it.

'And so is Halle Berry.'

It didn't take her long to find out what was going on. Of course, Holly and Bree were responsible. Some of the teenagers had brought along celebrity masks to wear at the Christmas party. The masks were very realistic, too realistic for the fool-proof new facial recognition system which was turning out to be not so fool-proof after all.

When Ferelith eventually sat back down at the computer, it immediately made the new sound again — twice. She looked at the screen and her eyes widened. Apparently, both Kim AND Kanye were staying at the hotel. That was going to make life very interesting.

15

The Queenie pub was heaving with people. Christmas music could be heard above the chatter and laughter and there was a festive spirit in the air. Everyone was having a good time.

In one corner, half a dozen members of the kitchen staff from the Manor were crammed round a little table. They had dropped by the Queenie after their shift. They had only intended to have a quick drink but, somehow, one drink had led to another. Then another. After all, it was Christmas. A burst of laughter went round the table.

'Well, you seem like a merry bunch.'

They looked round. Standing there was a very striking woman with a wide smile, a party hat and a cocktail glass complete with umbrella.

'We are a merry bunch,' retorted Kenny, one of the commis chefs. 'We've finished work for the day so now all we have to do is enjoy ourselves.'

The woman threw out her arms, some of her cocktail spilling over the side of the glass. A sort of awed silence fell over the group; they had all noticed how the movement pulled her slinky red dress even more tightly against her gorgeous body.

'If only I was with you,' she groaned. 'I'm here with my work Christmas party and it is — SO — BORING. Can you believe it, they're actually doing a quiz at the moment? A quiz — at a Christmas party! I couldn't bear it any longer. I must have the dreariest workmates in the world.'

There was a clamour of voices.

'Why don't you join us?'

She tried to focus on them all at the same time, her voice slurring slightly. 'Would you mind?'

'Of course not,' came a volley of replies.

They hurriedly made space for her but, rather to the disappointment of the others, she squeezed herself onto the bench between Kenny and the wall. She wriggled her bottom to settle herself and grinned. 'This is cosy.' Tossing back the remains of her drink, she held up her empty glass.

'More drink, we need more drink! Someone get another round in and this one's on me!'

A cheer went up and the next round was ordered. She looked at them blearily.

'So what do you lovely guys all do?'

'Guess,' said Kenny, his mind being sent into a whirl by her heady perfume. He could feel the warmth of her thigh. He wasn't at all sure what was happening but the situation was making him feel very happy.

She looked at him, her eyes swaying slightly, and he gulped. He had never been this close to such a bombshell before.

'Do you work in a restaurant?'

He blinked in surprise. 'How did you know?'

Her eyes narrowed. 'It's a burger joint,

isn't it? I can smell it on your clothes.'

There were howls of protest round the table. 'A burger joint?' someone cried. 'We work in the kitchen at Fosbury Manor! We're all chefs there.'

Her eyes widened. 'That posh hotel? I don't believe it. That's an amazing place.' She gazed at Kenny. 'You must be so good at what you do.'

Kenny felt himself blushing at the compliment.

'There's a lot of competition to get jobs there.'

She was looking at him in open admiration.

'I would love to work in a place like that. It must be fantastic.'

He laughed. 'I could tell you some stories. You wouldn't believe some of the things that are going on there at the moment.'

She leaned towards him. He could see flecks of purple amongst the blue of her pupils. His mind whirled some more.

'Tell me,' she murmured. 'What's it like?'

182

But then a gruff voice sounded from across the table. 'Now then, Kenny. We don't talk about work on our nights out.' It was an older man and his voice held a hint of warning.

Just for an instant, it seemed to Kenny that a flash of annoyance crossed the woman's face. But it was gone almost before it was there. She looked at him.

'Is that your name? Kenny?' He nodded. With a grin, she stood up and held out a hand. 'Well I'm Layanna, Kenny, and I'm pleased to meet you. Now let's go and dance!'

The pub's small dance floor was packed with revellers. Layanna and Kenny squeezed their way into the middle and made themselves some space. *Feliz Navidad* was playing and Layanna began singing along with the song at the top of her voice while wriggling and swaying as much as was possible in the circumstances. They kept being pressed together by the dancers around them which Layanna didn't seem to mind. It left Kenny feeling rather breathless.

The song came to an end and *Lonely This Christmas* began to play instead. The slow, seductive music left Kenny in a tizz of uncertainty as to how they should dance to it. But before he had time to come to a decision, Layanna had slipped into his arms. She pulled him close, her lips moving against his ear as she sang along, the two of them swaying together.

'So what's it like working at the Manor?' she murmured after a while. 'Is it really as brilliant there as people say?'

Kenny dragged his mind away from the glorious scent of her hair.

'We're not really allowed to discuss our work.'

There was a sad 'Oh,' in his ear. To his horror, Layanna moved a little away from him. He felt a rush of disappointment. Holding this extraordinary woman was such a wonderful sensation; it was surely what he had been put on Earth to experience?

'There must be something you can tell me. Is it true that Lyle Cranford is staying there?'

'Well . . .' Kenny said uncertainly.

Then Layanna was pressing up against him again. He felt a wave of dizzying excitement. Nothing about what was happening seemed possible. Now she was so close that their two bodies felt as if they were merging into one. An idea began dancing about in his head. If he carried on talking then perhaps she would carry on clinging to him. He tested the theory tentatively.

'It was the weirdest thing; Lyle Cranford took over the whole hotel for his family and friends . . .' Her arms tightened. *It was working*, he thought. *Keep talking!*

Quite a time passed before Layanna and Kenny returned to the little table.

'I'm parched,' Layanna groaned. 'Another round of drinks. I'm paying!'

'I think I've had enough,' the older man smiled.

But Layanna just hooted at him. 'No party poopers here!' she cried and the others joined in.

The drinks arrived and she kept trying

to steer the conversation onto the topic of the hotel.

'So what was going on with those penguins?' she asked. 'That was the strangest story.'

'You must have lots of famous people staying there. What are they like?'

'I'd love to see what it's like inside the hotel. Do you have any photos?'

But despite the fact that everyone round the table was relaxed and pleasantly drunk, they weren't at all forthcoming. Staff at the Manor seemed to have it ingrained in them not to talk about their work at hotel. What she had discovered from Kenny on the dancefloor seemed to be about as much as she was going to get.

She decided to change tack.

'I should be going; I need my beauty sleep.'

Kenny tried to think of a romantic response. Her hand touched his knee and squeezed it as if by accident. 'I need to call a taxi but my phone is out of charge. Could I borrow yours, sweetie?'

'Of course,' Kenny said, handing it to her. He was pleased. While she was on the phone, he'd have time to work out a subtle, sophisticated way of suggesting that they take the taxi together.

She got to her feet. 'It's a bit noisy here. I'll find somewhere quieter and be right back.'

Kenny watched her leave, all kinds of delightful possibilities swirling about in his mind.

However, the bright smile and dozy look dropped from Layanna's face as she hurried through the crowd to the pavement outside the pub. She was certain that all kinds of fascinating things were happening at the Manor and she was determined to find out what they were.

She flicked through the photos on Kenny's phone. There were any number of them but none seemed of much interest. But then her eyes narrowed; there was a file labelled 'From the Manor'. She hurriedly opened it. Most of the photos were taken in the kitchen and were of the food that was being prepared. There were some of Kenny's workmates but there seemed to be few, if any, of guests at the hotel. She grimaced in disappointment; she would need to return the phone to Kenny before he became suspicious.

But suddenly her finger froze. On the screen, there was a blurred picture which looked as if it was a CCTV image. She couldn't believe it. George Clooney's face was staring out at her. She hurriedly checked the date and time. The photo had been taken that morning.

Could he possibly be staying at the hotel? As her finger flicked eagerly on through the rest of the photos, she used her free hand to call a number on her own phone.

'News desk,' came a gruff voice.

'Hey, Derek, it's Layanna here. You won't believe the story that I've got . . .'

* * *

Ferelith was gripped by her dream. She was gazing at a huge green screen and on it were the blurred infra-red images of two people dancing. Somehow or other, she knew that they were herself and Geraint. The two of them were swirling about, their movements perfect, their footwork exquisite. But now they were slowing. Now they were standing in each other's arms. Now their faces were coming together. Now . . . now there was a strange chirruping sound.

'Groo,' she muttered and fumbled for her phone. She pulled off her sleep mask and gazed blearily at the screen. 'Hello Dad.'

'Sorry to disturb you, darling, but would you mind dropping by my office?' Ferelith tried to think but her mind seemed to be working through treacle.

'It's a quarter to six in the morning, Dad.'

'I'm afraid we have a situation on our hands.'

Ferelith was proud of herself. When she opened the door of her father's office, it wasn't even six o'clock yet. She wasn't exactly fresh as a daisy, but she was showered and dressed and her hair almost looked brushed.

Her father wasn't alone. Franklyn was speaking into his phone with a low but furious voice while Lyle was sprawled in a chair with newspapers scattered all around him.

Ferelith closed the door behind her.

'What's going on, Dad?'

Lionel looked at her wearily. 'It's the papers. Fosbury Manor is all over the front pages.'

16

Chief Inspector Ralph Ibbertson cut a frustrated figure. 'My concern is for public safety. Hundreds of people have gathered outside the hotel grounds and the crowd is growing.'

Lyle just shrugged. 'They seemed fairly good-natured to me. Are they doing any harm?'

'For a start, they're wandering about all over the road.'

Lyle looked at him curiously. 'So it's the traffic flow that concerns you rather than the crowd?' 'It's two days before Christmas and the police are already stretched to the limit,' the chief inspector snapped back. 'This is the last thing we need. You have to put out a statement, Mr Cranford. The people have gathered here because of those ridiculous newspaper stories. They think, quite wrongly, that the hotel is full of celebrities. You have got to make it clear that no one interesting is staying here at the moment.'

Lyle raised an eyebrow.

'I might take that personally, Chief Inspector.'

Ferelith's eyes suddenly widened.

'Dad — you're on TV!'

The television screen in the corner of Lionel's office was switched on, though it had been muted when the Chief Inspector had arrived. Ferelith quickly turned up the volume. Lionel was standing by the entrance of the Manor with the crowd in a lively mood behind him.

'It's the interview I did earlier,' he said but he was hurriedly hushed as the journalist pointing her microphone at him. 'So who is really staying at Fosbury Manor at the moment?' she asked.

'We never discuss our guests in public,' Lionel retorted. 'This is a hotel where people's privacy is respected.'

The journalist snorted. 'What happens at Fosbury Manor stays at Fosbury Manor?'

'If you like. Our guests expect the

highest standards of confidentiality from us. But I can assure you that the names being bandied about in the newspapers this morning are fanciful in the extreme. The journalists responsible for the stories have let their imaginations run away with them completely.'

'But there are photographs,' the journalist pressed him. 'Images from the hotel's own CCTV system showing the likes of George Clooney, Laura Dern and Kim Kardashian.'

Lionel shook his head. 'Have you seen the quality of the photographs? It's a nonsense. The people are barely recognisable.'

'Are you assuring us that none of those people are staying here?'

'As I said, we never discuss our guests.'

'But you're not denying they're staying here?'

'I'm neither admitting it nor denying it. This isn't a matter that I'm prepared to discuss.'

The journalist touched her ear; she was getting a message from her producer.

She turned to the camera with a dazzling smile. 'So that's the rather confusing situation here at Fosbury Manor Hotel in London. Back to the studio now.'

Marja and Tone, the programme's hosts, appeared on the screen. They were sitting on a sofa looking at each other curiously. 'What do you think?' Marja asked. 'This is just the sort of thing that Lyle Cranford would do — to pack a luxury hotel with his celebrity friends over Christmas.'

Tone nodded. 'And the manager wasn't very convincing. He's clearly hiding something. I reckon the celebrities really are there.'

Ferelith muted the TV and Chief Inspector Ibbertson turned angrily to Lionel.

'That's just made things worse! Why on earth didn't you state clearly that none of those celebrities is staying here?'

Lionel's cheeks flushed. 'We don't discuss our guests in public. It's a matter of principle.'

'I don't give a hoot about your

principles. Even more people are going to turn up now.' He pointed a finger at Lyle. 'You have got to put out a statement.'

Lyle shrugged. 'People wouldn't believe it.'

The Chief Inspector threw his hands into the air. 'So what do you intend to do?'

'When life gives you lemons, make lemonade.'

'Lemons? Now what are you talking about?'

Lyle turned to Franklyn, a grin on his face. 'I've had an idea.'

★ ★ ★

'DJ Klaws? Who's DJ Klaws?' Geraint asked.

Ferelith shook her head. 'The lead singer of Hi Heaven. You've surely heard of them?'

'Are they some sort of band?'

'They swept the board at the Grammys.'

'Oh right.' He thought to himself for a moment. 'I remember my mum really liking Val Doonican.'

Ferelith gazed at him in disbelief. 'You need taking in hand.'

He grinned. 'Are you applying for the job?'

There was a silence. He had been joking, of course. But now the words hung in the air between them. Ferelith felt herself flushing. She couldn't imagine anything she would like more.

The silence stretched. Neither of them seemed to know how to move the conversation on. It was a difficult moment. Geraint cleared his throat.

'Anyway, so this DJ Klaws and his band are putting on a free concert at the Manor this afternoon?'

Ferelith nodded. 'They're in the middle of a European tour but Lyle is flying them in from Amsterdam specially.'

Geraint looked at her in befuddlement. 'You never know where you are with him, do you?'

Lionel had been horrified when Lyle

had come up with the idea. Chief Inspector Ibbertson hadn't been best pleased either. But their objections had been carried off on a whirlwind of enthusiasm from Lyle. 'Think of it as a surprise present for all those good people who have gathered at the hotel in the hope of seeing some celebrities. Nobody should be disappointed at Christmas. There may not be any celebrities staying here but we'll have a celebrity concert instead.'

Ferelith had noticed Franklyn discussing the matter urgently with Lyle in a low voice. He wasn't the sort of person to be troubled in the slightest by the crowd's disappointment. However, he did care a great deal about the GroupChat business. She suspected that his interest was in the welcome publicity that a surprise concert would generate for the company just before it unveiled the biggest product launch in its history.

However, she had little time to think about any of that. The staff were suddenly faced with having to cope with a concert being arranged in the hotel's grounds that afternoon from scratch.

The days at Fosbury Manor normally progressed in an atmosphere of unerring efficiency. The hotel's facilities were of the very highest quality, the staff knew their jobs perfectly and everything was designed to ensure that each guest had a stay of unrivalled quality and enjoyment.

But ever since Lyle and his party had arrived, the hotel's routines had been tossed into the air. The decision to hold a concert in the grounds on the spur of the moment swept away any last vestiges of organisation.

Lyle had brought in a management company, Fluorescent Momentz, to arrange the concert. The first Ferelith knew of it was the arrival of a gaudi-ly-painted travel trailer full of people shouting into phones. That was followed by a stream of trucks, out of which an army of workers appeared. They set up the stage on the lawn so quickly that it seemed grow before their eyes. More trucks arrived laden with portable toilets, causing Erik to give a shriek of outrage when he spotted them. Then there were all kinds of concession stands; burger bars, ice cream vans, face-painting stalls, even a temporary hot-tub. Ferelith shuddered to think how that might be used.

Meanwhile Lyle had ordered a continuous stream of the kitchen's Christmas dainties to be distributed amongst the people on the street around the Manor. The police, having given up the unequal struggle, had closed the road to traffic and it was now filled with a party atmosphere. And as news spread that a free concert was to take place at the Manor, the crowd grew and grew.

Ferelith only saw all this in glimpses. She found herself rushing from one place to another, helping to deal with the inevitable problems. She had begun to hate her phone's chirpy ringtone. At one point she caught up with Geraint and his team who were hurriedly putting up barriers to stop the most precious parts of the grounds from being overwhelmed later.

'I hate to think what sort of state the

place is going to be in tomorrow,' she said miserably.

Geraint forced a weak smile onto his face.

'But it's making Lyle happy. This is Fosbury Manor. What the guests want . . .'

But he couldn't finish. Ferelith could sense his upset at what was happening to his beloved grounds. Without thinking, she stepped forward and wrapped him in a hug. 'It'll be all right.'

His arms went round her. 'Of course it will.'

It was only meant to be a quick hug. But as they stood there together, Ferelith found that she couldn't let him go. It was just too lovely to be holding him and to be held.

There was a sort of shuddering rumble which Ferelith had never experienced in her life before. The ground beneath them seemed to vibrate. Her eyes widened. She had heard about the earth moving but this was extraordinary.

'Good grief,' Geraint muttered. He

pulled back from her and Ferelith looked up. A huge helicopter was slowly descending onto the lawn. DJ Klaws and his band had arrived.

★ ★ ★

It was a brilliant concert, Ferelith thought. There had been no chance for a rehearsal and the lighting, organised at the last minute, was haphazard at times. But DJ Klaws knew how to put on a show and, from the first notes of *Rock! Rock!* to the last sweet chorus of *My Alabamalama*, he and the rest of the crew had the crowd in a state of joyous delirium.

She got to it all a bit late. The band had decided to stay the night, which was a problem as the hotel was full. But Lyle had persuaded some of his guests to move to a hastily-created dormitory in a conference suite so that some rooms could be given over to DJ Klaws and his colleagues. Naturally, that took quite a bit of organising.

By the time Ferelith was finally free, the concert was well under way and the crowd was dancing and singing along happily with the music. Before she joined them, she scoured the grounds for Geraint. She found him placing last-minute fencing round the sensory garden. He was reluctant to leave the work unfinished but she gave him no choice.

'You have to come, Geraint. You'll never get a chance like this again.' And taking his hand, she dragged him round to the front of the hotel to where the concert was taking place.

It took him a while to relax but gradually he became infected by the mood of the crowd. He even danced with her. At some point, she felt his arm go round her shoulders. She thought it was probably because there was quite a crush and he didn't want them to get separated. But the arm stayed there even when the crush eased.

The final song, *My Alabamalama*, was one of Ferelith's favourites. She sang along with DJ Klaws and the crowd and Geraint held her tightly.

At the end, everyone was cheering and calling out for more. It was such a moment of celebration. She found the two of them were facing each other and that he was cupping her cheeks.

Then with a sense of amazement, mixed in with the realisation that she had known that this was going to happen from the moment they had first met, she felt Geraint kissing her.

17

The dawn sky in the distance was being lightened by delicate streaks of colour and everything was quiet as Ferelith jogged along the path. All she could hear was her steady breathing and the sound of her feet padding against the ground. Her cheeks had become moistened by a faint mist in the air but she was glowing inside.

When the concert had ended, she and Geraint had been whirled apart. There was no time to think about anything apart from getting the Manor back into some kind of order.

The organisers had been very efficient. The crowd was quickly dispersed and, by midnight, the security team was doing a sweep of the grounds to make sure that the only people left were hotel staff and guests. The stalls had been packed up and driven away. Litter-gatherers had appeared from somewhere and got to work. The sound and lighting equipment had been taken down and disappeared. Now, the only thing left to do was dismantle the stage and that was due to happen first thing in the morning.

She wasn't sure when she had got to bed; around two in the morning, she thought. But Lionel had been glad that they had managed to get back on top of things.

'Let's just hope that the concert is the last of the Christmas surprises,' he had said as he wished her goodnight.

That had made her laugh out loud.

'Don't bet on it.'

It had been a very long day. But as she lay in bed, she couldn't get to sleep. That moment when Geraint had turned to her and kissed her was going round and round in her head on a loop. It had been so sweet and lovely.

The two of them hadn't really talked afterwards. There was too much noise at the end of the concert. And then they had been so busy with the rest of the staff at the hotel. There hadn't been the chance to slip off for a quiet cuddle and to whisper nonsense to each other.

At one point as Ferelith had lain there in bed, she had stretched over to the little table and picked up her phone. She looked at it, wondering if she should send a message to Geraint. She longed to do so but something held her back. She felt strangely shy and uncertain.

She wasn't sure how he felt. Was it possible he had just been caught up in the excitement of the moment? Perhaps he even regretted kissing her. Though as he held her in his arms, regret had seemed to be the last thing he was feeling. She closed her eyes and relived it one more time.

* * *

'So you're not a DJ Klaws fan, Erik?' Ferelith grinned.

'Mr Klaws is a guest at the hotel and I naturally hold him in the utmost respect,' Erik retorted loftily. His upper lip twitched. 'Though it's true I've yet to develop a full appreciation for his music.'

'In other words, you hate it?'

'I'm sure that it has many sterling qualities which I am still to discover.'

'He certainly knows how to enjoy himself,' Ferelith said ruefully. The suite in which DJ Klaws was staying was directly above reception and, even though it was barely nine in the morning, they could hear music pounding through the ceiling. Miss Buckley-Tone on the grand piano was bravely trying to compete with her gentle Christmas carols but it was an uneven struggle.

'I'm rather at a loss as to what to do,' Erik said in bafflement. 'People playing loud music in their rooms isn't something that happens at the Manor.'

The light fitting above them seem to shiver at a particularly noisy drum-roll.

'It's happening now,' Ferelith retorted.

'Normally I would request that the racket be lowered to a more acceptable level as it was upsetting neighbouring guests. But in this case, the guests are having as much fun as he is.'

'Is that what's happening?' Ferelith asked curiously. 'There's a party going on?'

Erik nodded. 'And the kitchen is hard at work supplying them with all kinds of bizarre requests. Who eats oysters for breakfast, for heaven's sake?' His lips pursed in disapproval. 'And there are television cameras everywhere.'

Ferelith frowned. 'I thought the journalists and media folk were long gone?'

Erik shook his head. 'These are his own people. Apparently, he has a cable show in America. The cameras follow him wherever he goes so that every incident in his life can be recorded and shown to his adoring masses.'

Ferelith looked at Erik in horror. 'I would hate that. What about his privacy?'

'I suspect that's why the wild party is happening. Mr Klaws has a reputation to maintain. Still, he's a guest at the hotel and if that's what he wants . . .' Erik frowned and turned to her. 'Incidentally, have you seen Geraint yet this morning?'

Ferelith felt a flush warming her

cheeks. She had been thinking about him almost continually but she hadn't actually seen him.

'Why do you ask?' she said casually. She suddenly wondered if the two of them had been spotted kissing at the concert. That would prompt even more rumours amongst the staff.

But Erik was shaking his head.

'I'm just feeling rather sorry for him and his team. The grounds are in a terrible state.'

Ferelith sighed. 'They are, aren't they?'

It wasn't just the people trampling all over the place at the concert; it was innumerable vans and lorries too. They hadn't been too careful about where they went and now much of the grounds were a churned-up mess of fake snow and mud.

'It's going to be such a lot of work for them to get it back into its usual state.'

'It's going to cost money too,' Erik added.

A delivery driver in a blue uniform appeared through the doors of the hotel pushing a trolley filled with all kinds of packages. He parked it by the reception desk and looked curiously up at the ceiling. 'What's happening at the Manor? It sounds like party central going on here today.'

Erik just sighed and held up a hand.

'Don't go there.' He peered over the desk at the contents of the trolley. 'So what's all this?'

The driver looked at his clipboard. 'It's a whole bunch of parcels for a Mr Klaws.' He peered at the name with a frown. 'This isn't some sort of Christmas joke, is it?'

'I'm afraid not,' Erik said wearily. 'Can we keep the trolley for the time being?'

'No problem. I'll collect it again next time.' He lifted his phone, taking a photo as confirmation that his parcels had been delivered. 'Smile, please.' Ferelith did so, though she suspected Erik didn't. 'Thanks. Have a good Christmas.'

'And you,' the two of them called after him.

Erik wandered round to the front of

the desk and peered at the parcels.

'I shudder to think what's in these. But I'll get a porter to take them upstairs.'

Ferelith shook her head. 'No need. I'll do it.'

Erik lifted an eyebrow. 'We have some ear-plugs if you would like.'

The lift gave a cheerful beep and its doors slid open. Ferelith began to push the trolley out but then she stopped in astonishment.

It was as if the whole of the hotel's first floor had become one big party. There were people everywhere wandering in and out of each other's rooms. Children were running around, champagne bottles were being waved, there was chatter and laughter. And through it all, music boomed from one of the suites at the end of the corridor; she could feel the vibrations through the floor. She shook her head slowly. It didn't seem possible that this was happening at the Manor.

She made slow progress with the trolley along the corridor, constantly having to apologise to the people blocking her way. But no one minded moving; they were all having such a good time.

'Ferelith!' came a shout. Holly and Bree rushed up to her. 'Are you here to join the party?'

'Working, I'm afraid,' she said. 'I'm looking for DJ Klaws. Have you seen him?'

Bree pointed. 'That's Party HQ. We got a selfie with him, it's amazing.' She held out her phone in excitement. 'Shall I show you?'

Ferelith smiled. 'Maybe later.'

'And he said we could join his band one day,' Holly added eagerly. 'I'm going to be on bass guitar and Bree will be on the drums.'

'I'll look forward to that,' Ferelith laughed. She pushed on with the trolley. 'Enjoy yourselves.'

She wasn't quite sure what to expect but the suite, when she came to it, was something of a surprise. The music was actually coming from a neighbouring room and, instead of being filled with noisy chaos, DJ Klaws' own room was

212

rather peaceful. There were plenty of people, including the other members of the band, but they were chatting quietly. DJ himself, wearing a dressing gown, slippers and glasses, was in an armchair reading a newspaper with a cup of tea at his side.

He glanced over the top of his glasses as the trolley appeared and, at once, his eyes lit up.

'That's what we're looking for.' Folding the paper neatly and putting it down, he got to his feet and held out his hand with a smile. 'Hi there, I'm Donald Klaws. Call me DJ.'

'Ferelith,' she smiled.

'Now that's a lovely name.' He looked at her thoughtfully. 'You wouldn't mind helping us with a scene, would you, Ferelith?'

'A scene?'

He nodded to a couple of cameramen who were readying their equipment. 'For my reality TV show back home, *DJ On The Spin*. Have you seen it?'

'Well . . .'

'It's Christmas Eve and the band needs to be seen to be partying. Are you all right with that?'

'Er . . .'

'These parcels are some new costumes for me and the band but don't worry about that; they're for later. All you need to do is make your entrance again and then go with the flow.'

'Make my entrance again?' She was getting more confused by the minute. However, an assistant ushered her out of the room with the trolley and began to give her a stream of instructions. The music in the neighbouring room was switched off and, moments later, different music started up from DJ Klaws's room. With a 'Smile, now — you're on camera!' the assistant gave her the signal. Beaming for all she was worth, Ferelith pushed the trolley back into the room with a lively 'Parcels for DJ Klaws!'

The scene in the room had completely changed. DJ and the band were now in their familiar leather gear — the slippers and glasses had gone — and they seemed to be in the middle of a jam session.

When DJ spotted her, he hurriedly stopped it. The music died away and he gazed at her in awe.

'Wow — you British babes are gorgeous!' He began to fan himself with a sheet of music.

'Are we?' Ferelith said uncertainly.

'Music — give us music, guys,' DJ cried and, with the cameramen recording everything, the music started up again; but this time it was dramatic, sensuous tango music.

DJ strode up to Ferelith, took her firmly in his arms, and began leading her in a dance around the room. 'Goodness,' she gasped.

He gave her a quick wink. 'Don't worry, it's just a bit of fun for the cameras,' he murmured.

Before she could reply, he had done a very neat slide past an armchair and was whirling her out onto the balcony where another cameraman was waiting. 'Why did I never come to London before?' he called out. 'This is a city of angels!'

He suddenly moved forward so that she had to grab him tightly to stop herself doing a triple somersault over the railings.

'You gorgeous thing,' he growled, moving in close but carefully keeping his profile to the camera. Ferelith gazed up at him in shock; she wasn't at all sure what was about to happen next. And then, from the corner of her eye, she caught a glimpse of Geraint, holding a battered-looking poinsettia, gazing up in horror.

18

Ferelith turned in her chair and gazed wearily at the security room. She was surrounded by the gifts which Lyle had brought with him to be given to his guests at the Christmas Eve party.

Of course, they were amazing and Ferelith shuddered to think how much the contents of the room were worth at that moment. But it was her job to ensure there was a gift for every guest, all correctly labelled and packaged. And she couldn't seem to focus her mind on the task.

She kept thinking of Geraint. He had looked so horrified earlier when he had seen her with DJ Klaws on the balcony. The sight of his face gazing up at them had seared itself on her memory.

Of course, nothing had actually happened. She had clung desperately onto DJ Klaws for her own safety as he had moved closer and closer, murmuring nonsense. But just as it seemed that he must be about to kiss her, someone had called 'Cut!' in the background and DJ Klaws had immediately released her and made sure she was steady on her feet. He had turned to the cameraman. 'How did the scene look?'

'Pretty decent, I think,' the cameraman murmured. Back in the room, DJ Klaws had put on his glasses and a huddle of them had gathered round the camera. After looking through the clip a couple of times, DJ Klaws had nodded. 'That looks fine and the sound quality is good. Tidy it into a thirty-second video clip and put it out on social media straight away.' The group scattered and he turned to Ferelith with a smile. 'You come across well on camera, Ferelith. Very natural.'

She gazed at him in confusion.

'I don't understand. What just happened?'

'That will go out as a teaser clip on social media to encourage people to tune into our regular cable-cast later today.'

'You and me dancing?'

The corner of his mouth twitched.

'DJ Klaws has a reputation to uphold. When he sees a beautiful woman, he can't help but make a move on her. It's what his audience expects.'

For a moment, Ferelith was distracted by the thought that she had just been described as a beautiful woman by an international celebrity. Though it was odd how he spoke as if DJ Klaws was somehow separate to himself.

'Thanks for that, Ferelith,' he said, shaking her hand with a smile. There was no sign of the passionate eyes which had burned into hers just seconds before. He was like an actor moving in and out of character. 'I appreciate your help.'

'Er, my pleasure,' she replied in a daze.

'It's set things up nicely for the next part of the drama.'

She pushed the now empty trolley back through the partying crowds in the passageway. She supposed that it would be a good story to tell her friends but she kept thinking of Geraint gazing at the two of them on the balcony. He had looked so miserable. She would have to seek him out and explain everything; just as soon as she had a spare moment.

* * *

Wearily, Ferelith put the parcel she had been checking into one of the big red sacks and ticked off another name on her list. The Christmas Eve party would be beginning in a matter of hours. It was always the highlight of the festive celebrations at the Manor but she couldn't get herself into the spirit of things at all.

She felt so upset and confused. Those moments with Geraint at the concert the night before seemed like a lifetime ago. She had felt in such a whirl of happiness. She had been sure it was the start of something special between the two of them. But now all she could think about was the expression on his face as he had looked up at the balcony. She had to speak to him. But there was so much to do.

She looked at the mountain of parcels and her eyes narrowed. A surge of determination went through her. She would give it a blitz and get the job finished. Then she could find Geraint and explain what had happened in DJ Klaws's room. Everything would be fine again.

She grabbed the next parcel and reached out to the tape dispenser. But then she grimaced; it had run out. She got to her feet.

'Erik, do you have a spare roll of sticky tape?'

'I believe so, Miss Ferelith.' He peered under the counter.

But all thoughts of parcels and sticky tape were suddenly swept from Ferelith's mind. Geraint had appeared in the doorway of the hotel carrying a tray of Christmas cacti. He caught sight of her and his feet slowed to a stop. The two of them gazed at each other. The anguished look on his face was so painful to her. However, a slow change came over his expression. There was a sort of melting. A sense that something precious and dear was beginning to flow between them across the hall. Just for an instant, she thought that he was about to move towards her. It was what she wanted more than anything in the world.

But, suddenly, all of that was forgotten. Through the entrance of the Manor, an extraordinary-looking woman had just appeared. Striding past Geraint with two cameramen in her wake, she came to a stop in the middle of the reception area and struck a dramatic pose.

'Where's — that — TROLLOP?' she demanded in a voice which echoed off the walls. The hall fell into absolute silence. 'Where's that vixen who is trying to steal my man?'

Ferelith knew who she was. Actress, film director, professional drama queen and renowned squeeze of DJ Klaws, Myrmalette C. Mee was one of the most recognisable women in the world.

She stood there in her flowing designer dress which clung to her in remarkable ways and gazed about with eyes blazing in fury.

A sense of dread gripped Ferelith. Could this have something to do with her scene earlier on the balcony with DJ Klaws? Although she didn't appear to have been spotted, it seemed to Ferelith that Myrmalette knew exactly where she was. With the cameras recording everything, the moment was being drawn out exquisitely slowly for dramatic purposes. She felt helpless with fear, like a rabbit about to be spotted by a fox. She could only stare at this astonishing woman whose every movement was a pose and whose hair was piled high on her head. How did she manage that? Ferelith wondered vaguely. Did she have a hairdresser travelling with her?

All at once, Myrmalette's eyes lit upon Ferelith. It was as if a bolt of electricity had struck the woman. She shuddered. Stepped back. Tottered on her enormous heels. Every man in the room seemed to take an instinctive step forward to help, even Erik. But somehow she gathered her strength and drew herself up to her full height.

'There — she — is!' she cried, pointing at Ferelith with a finger encased by dazzling rings. 'There's the she-devil who seeks to rip the very soul from my body!'

All eyes in the room turned to Ferelith with outrage. She felt herself blushing and stammering,

'No . . . but... it wasn't . . . I didn't . . .'

Myrmalette didn't have the slightest interest in what Ferelith had to say. There was only one star in this drama. Striding over, she fixed Ferelith with a fearful glare. Waiting for a moment to let the cameras catch up, she then let rip. 'This woman has taken my tiny precious heart in her hands and has shredded it to pieces before the entire world,' she began and she took it from there.

If it wasn't for the fact that the torrent of fury was directed at her, Ferelith would have been impressed. Myrmalette C. Mee wasn't the most subtle of actresses but she knew how to deliver a line. As her voice rose and fell, surged and whirled, the hall seemed to overflow with the crashing waves of her emotions.

It occurred to Ferelith at some point that the words had clearly been written for her and they were certainly well rehearsed. However, the performance was none the less powerful for that.

'Has there ever existed such a demon?' Myrmalette cried out in anguish to the ceiling. 'This monstrous horror who would rend apart two innocent souls?'

It went on and on with no one in the hall daring to interrupt. Ferelith was left feeling like some disgusting bug discovered in a picnic hamper.

Then she caught sight of Geraint. He was transfixed by Myrmalette's words, his face pale with shock. To her horror, Ferelith realised that he had been taken in by her.

'Nooo!' she wanted to cry to him across the hall, perhaps clutching her heart pitifully as Myrmalette might do. 'It's all nonsense, Geraint. Nothing happened!' But she couldn't manage it. Like everyone else, she was stunned into awed silence by the power of Myrmalette's presence.

All at once, there was a kerfuffle at the other side of the hall. DJ Klaws had appeared surrounded by his own cameras. Turning and spotting him, Myrmalette uttered a shriek which made everyone in the hall wince. Clutching a hand to her forehead, she cried out 'Betrayed!' and sank elegantly to the floor.

Ferelith was beginning to understand how things worked in the world of reality TV, so she wasn't entirely surprised when DJ Klaws then uttered his own cry of despair. He rushed over to Myrmalette and threw himself to his knees beside her. He took her in his arms in a way that kept her lovely profile visible and proceeded with his own speech. He cried out tearfully that he should be given one last chance and promised that, if she forgave him, he would be faithful to her for ever.

As the speech came to an end, Myrmalette slowly woke from her faint.

'Where is this place?' she called, looking around in unconvincing confusion. She produced a tiny lace handkerchief to dab gracefully at her dry eyes and DJ Klaws kissed the back of her hand fervently and raised her to her feet.

But then he sank dramatically back down to his knees and produced from his pocket the chunkiest diamond ring Ferelith had ever seen. Washing the dishes would be tricky with something like that on your finger, she thought, though possibly Myrmalette didn't do the dishes very often.

DJ Klaws threw his arms into the air, holding on tightly to the ring.

'Myrmalette, will you do me the greatest honour in my life and become my wife?' he said.

Myrmalette uttered another, even louder, shriek and fainted again but not before DJ Klaws had caught her in her arms as she had cried out, 'Yes, my darling, yes!'

And as it turned out, she recovered quickly enough to watch in satisfaction as the ring was being put on her finger and to give her eyes a few more unnecessary dabs.

The rest passed in a blur. Encouraged by one of Myrmalette's minions, the watching guests burst into enthusiastic applause as the engaged couple made their way outside. They were met by a tornado of exploding fireworks and popping champagne corks before leaving in a huge helicopter trailing plumes of pink and blue smoke.

'What just happened?' Ferelith muttered. It felt as if she was waking up out of some mad dream. Then a thought came rushing into her head.

'Geraint!' she gasped. She hurriedly turned. But he was walking off across the lawn, his shoulders slumped in misery.

19

The music stopped suddenly. Wild cheers of excitement rose up as the two women raced across the ballroom. One made a desperate dive but slipped and fell spread-eagled across the chair. The other plumped down on top of her and raised her hands in victory.

Ferelith looked on in disbelief as the two of them in their elegant party dresses began to wrestle. She had never seen a game of Musical Chairs like it. They were shrieking with laughter, arms and legs going everywhere.

A look of panic had fallen over the Party-Meister's face. He rushed forward, microphone in hand, and hurriedly inserted himself between the battling contestants.

'I think we have two winners, folks,' he announced to the cheering crowd. 'Let's have a huge round of applause as we give star prizes to both Sheila and

Charmaine!'

The cheers redoubled as two bottles of champagne were produced from somewhere. Untangling themselves, the contestants returned to their tables arm-in-arm, walking rather unsteadily but both well pleased.

The Party-Meister held up a hand and the noise lessened a little.

'Now, if my hard-working helpers could clear the chairs from the floor, we'll have a Christmas Hokey-Cokey in just a minute.'

Ferelith and two other members of staff moved forward and got to work.

'Remember, children, our Pin-The-Tail-On-The-Reindeer competition is still under way. There's a delicious Christmas dainty for every entrant and a state-of-the-art game console for the winner. And gentlemen, we're also looking for more contestants for our Guess-The-Christmas-Knobbly-Knees contest later to be compered by our wonderful host, Mr Lyle Cranford!'

Applause reverberated round the

room and Lyle stood up for a moment, waving and smiling.

It had been a brilliant Christmas Eve party, Ferelith had to admit. Not that she had been in a mood for it. All she wanted was to be able to explain to Geraint that nothing had happened between her and DJ Klaws. But his imagination had clearly got to work after he saw the two of them on the balcony. Then Myrmalette's mad accusations had only made the situation worse.

However, the hotel was in turmoil as the staff desperately tried to get things back to normal after DJ and his party had left. Then there was the Christmas Eve party to prepare for. There had been a million things needing doing and there hadn't been a moment for her to find Geraint.

It hadn't helped that there had been an issue with the GroupChat phones. They had urgently needed a software update to fix the problem with the batteries. Lyle had insisted on it being done immediately with every phone being gathered up and plugged into the strange-looking battery charger which was situated in a cloakroom. Many younger guests had been reluctant to hand their phones over and it had taken an age before the phones were all accounted for and the updating could begin. However eventually it was done and the party got underway.

The Party-Meister had proved an able organiser. He had led the guests in a mixture of traditional games, music and non-stop fun. The extensive Christmas buffet had proved very popular and those who found the excitement a bit much had been able to slip off to the bar next door where they could celebrate their Christmas Eve rather more peaceably.

Through it all, Ferelith's thoughts had kept drifting back to Geraint. Those sweet moments with him at the concert only the night before seemed a lifetime ago.

'WooooooooOOOOOOOOOOH-OH, the Hokey-Cokey!'

Ferelith watched with a faint smile as

the guests surged forwards and backwards. Lyle was right at the heart of it all, of course. He was clearly having a wonderful time as he had been all evening.

But then she caught sight of Erik; he was signalling to her from the door of the ballroom. She hurried over.

'The great man has arrived,' he murmured. 'He's changed into his costume and everything is ready.'

'Good for Dandy; that's perfect timing,' Ferelith said. 'I'll give you a signal when it's time for him to make his entrance.'

She hurried over to the Party-Meister and passed on the message. He held up his thumb and Ferelith returned to the door and positioned herself so that Erik could see her.

'Brilliant work, everyone,' the Party-Meister called out as the dance came to a riotous conclusion. 'I have rarely seen the Hokey-Cokey performed with such elegance and style. But now I have just received some very exciting news. A special visitor is on his way.'

There was a rush of excitement round the room. A large wooden chair gloriously decorated with tinsel and baubles was waiting beside the ballroom's Christmas tree. The younger children hurriedly gathered around it, barely able to contain themselves.

Ferelith dimmed the lights as the Party-Meister spoke into his microphone in a dramatic whisper.

'Quiet now, everyone. If we listen very carefully, we might be able to hear him arrive.'

Absolute silence fell over them. Ferelith couldn't believe the difference in the room. Only moments before, it had been filled with noisy chaos. She nodded to Erik and he raised a hand.

Then moments later there came a joyous 'Ho — Ho — Ho!' that seemed to overflow with fun.

Ferelith barely recognised Dandy Barham as he appeared in his Father Christmas outfit, carrying a huge bag of presents over his shoulder. He seemed larger than life somehow, his eyes above the curly white beard sparking with laughter.

'Ho — Ho — Ho!' he cried again, raising his free hand in greeting. 'A very Merry Christmas to you all, my friends. Ho — Ho — Ho!'

Wild cheers and applause swept him through the eager crowd and towards the decorated chair, surrounded by excited children. He shook hands and blew kisses and ho-ho-hoed with all his might. Meanwhile, three elves looking suspiciously like members of the hotel staff followed behind with more bags of presents.

Sinking into the chair, he picked up a tiny child with a mass of blonde hair and settled her comfortably on his knee. He turned to the guests.

'Well, my friends, you wouldn't believe what I've been through to get here.'

He proceeded to tell a completely mad story about his journey from the North Pole. Things had started going wrong when a helicopter flying past had surrounded the sleigh in pink and blue smoke so that they had lost their way. Then there had been a disaster over Belgium when Rudolph's red nose had fallen into a field of tomatoes and it had taken ages for them to find it again. Mrs Claus insisted on being dropped off as they were passing Birmingham because she wanted to be first in line for the Boxing Day Sales. Then Dancer had been headhunted by a producer on *Strictly* and they'd had to manage the rest of the journey without him. There had been one disaster after another but, thankfully, a Christmas miracle had occurred and the sleigh had arrived at the Manor.

Dandy was a natural story-teller and his tale had the whole room helpless with laughter. But then he then got down to the real business of the evening; handing out the presents.

Ferelith was still in awe at the stunning nature of the gifts and at the thought of how much they must all have cost. Though all Lyle cared about was that they brought some Christmas joy into the lives of the people he loved.

Dandy was a marvel as Father Christmas. As he handed the presents out, he had a word and a joke for everyone. Ferelith was amazed by how he managed it, given that he'd already had a long day at the theatre.

While the gifts were being distributed her mind inevitably drifted back to Geraint. She imagined he had gone home hours ago and she didn't suppose she would see him again until Boxing Day at the earliest, possibly not even then. The thought of the situation between them not being resolved for days filled her with a chill misery.

She couldn't really grasp how it had happened. The kisses they had shared at the end of the concert now seemed as insubstantial as a moment from a dream. It had been so wonderful but now everything had gone horribly wrong. And she had no idea how it was going to be put right.

'Thank you for your wonderful welcome, my friends, but it's time for me to go. The reindeer and I have a busy night ahead!' Dandy Barham was on his feet, being cheered and applauded to the rafters. He made his way slowly through the crowd, leading them in a rousing version of *We Wish You A Merry Christmas* and posing for selfies with virtually every step.

'Dandy, that was fantastic,' Ferelith said as she led him to the cloakroom to change. 'There's a whisky of your choice waiting for you at the bar. And I've had strict instructions from Mr Cranford — you're to take the bottle home with you.'

His eyes widened. 'That's a generous offer.'

Ferelith smiled. 'Mr Cranford is a very generous man.'

'Will you join me for a drink?' he asked.

Ferelith grimaced. 'I'm not sure I have time, Dandy. There's so much needing doing.'

'Just a quick one,' he prompted her. His eyes narrowed. 'You look as if you need cheering up.'

Ferelith felt herself flush. 'A quick one, then.'

Once Dandy was back in his ordinary clothes, Ferelith took him to the bar where they were soon provided with drinks. He looked at her closely.

'So why are those pretty eyes of yours looking so sad?'

Ferelith wasn't sure how to answer.

'Is it a matter of the heart?'

Tears welled up unprompted.

'It usually is.' He picked up his tumbler and held it out to her. They clinked glasses. 'To love in all its pain and glory.'

They sipped their drinks.

'Do you love him?' Dandy asked quietly.

This time, the tears spilled down her cheeks.

'I think I do,' she said in a shaky whisper.

He brought a perfectly laundered handkerchief from his top pocket and handed it to her.

'Let me give you a piece of advice, my dear, from someone whose heart has been broken more times than I care to remember. Grab opportunities for love whenever they come your way. Life is too short to waste them.'

Now Ferelith was crying freely.

'It's such a mess. I don't know what to do.'

He looked at her for a long, thoughtful moment.

'I never did give you a present, did I?'

He looked round. Attached to the nearby pillar of the bar was a bouquet of mistletoe. He reached out and snapped off a small sprig. Lifting it above their heads, he leaned forward and kissed her cheek. Then he held the mistletoe out to her.

'Now pass that on.' 'Merry Christmas, Ferelith.'

'And to you, Dandy.'

He wrapped her in a warm hug.

'Don't worry, things will work out for you and Geraint.'

She watched as the taxi drove off down the drive and thought that there are some people whom you just get on with and Dandy had been like that. They had sat together at the bar, she had told him about Geraint and, somehow, the two of them had become friends.

The taxi turned the corner and disappeared off down the road. She felt that she would like to return the favour some day. She would take Dandy out for a drink and offer him a sympathetic ear as he told her all about his worries. The corner of her mouth twitched; she suspected that he would have some colourful ones.

But it had helped her to talk to him. As she had done so, her thoughts and feelings had become clearer in her head.

It was the first time she had admitted to anyone, even to herself, that she loved Geraint. But she realised now just how true it was, and the admission made things much simpler. When you loved someone and there was a problem then you sorted it out.

A vague frown of uncertainty creased her forehead. But how? It was almost eleven o'clock on Christmas Eve. Geraint would have gone home hours ago. He probably wouldn't be back at work at the hotel for at least another couple of days. She couldn't bear to have the situation hanging on unresolved between them for that length of time; she needed to speak to him face to face.

It occurred to her that it would be easy enough to find out where he lived from the hotel's personnel files. But could she just turn up on his doorstep on Christmas Day?

Anyway, she didn't want to leave things until tomorrow. She wanted to sort them out with him now!

The thoughts whirled in her head. She had to do something but she didn't know what. She turned uncertainly to go back into the hotel but, as she did so, something caught her eye. In the gardens, she could see a light and a figure moving about. Her eyes widened in shock. It was Geraint.

20

Ferelith blinked. It didn't seem possible. But it really was him. She hadn't bothered to put on her coat to say goodbye to Dandy, but she didn't care as she hurried across the lawn.

She slowed as she approached him. Although it was dark, it was easy enough to see. There were lights from the hotel, and from the distant streets, and from the decorations round the oak tree. Also, Geraint was wearing a yellow helmet with a torch attached to it, like a miner's helmet. He had his back to her and he was walking slowly about the flower beds, leaning down to peer at things and making notes on the tablet in his hand.

Ferelith came to a stop, feeling suddenly uncertain. This was the first time she had spoken to him since the end of the concert. She had felt so happy. There had been a whirl of joy inside her at the memory of their kisses and the thought of what the future might hold. But then, everything had become horribly messy and confused.

She cleared her throat. 'Hi, Geraint.'

Her voice took him by surprise; he had clearly been deep in thought. She searched his face as he turned, trying to get some hint of his feelings. He was frowning, though that might have been caused by whatever he was doing.

'Evening, Ferelith.' He smiled slightly but perhaps that was simply politeness. 'Is the party finished, then?'

She nodded. 'Things are breaking up now. It seemed to go well.'

A silence fell, neither of them quite sure what to say. Ferelith felt dismay drifting over her. That was the thing she had always liked about Geraint; being with him had felt so natural. But now that seemed to have changed.

Somewhere at the back of her mind, a little voice was calling out to her, *Tell him, Ferelith. Tell him that you love him. Tell him that you're longing to throw your arms around him and kiss him. Tell him that you want to be with him for the rest of your life!* But she was scared. What if that wasn't what he wanted? What if what had happened at the concert had just been a passing moment and he wasn't really interested in her romantically? She didn't think she could bear that.

'What are you doing?' she eventually asked.

He gestured at the flower-beds.

'There's so much needing doing to get the grounds back up to standard. I'm just trying to make an assessment of the situation.'

'At eleven o'clock on Christmas Eve?'

He shrugged. 'I needed to be doing something. Otherwise, I'd just be sitting at home thinking about . . .' His voice tailed off. He frowned and looked down at his tablet. 'I'm just making some notes. I want to make a list of priorities for when the team gets back to work.'

His answer only prompted more questions in Ferelith's mind. But she didn't know how to ask.

'Perhaps I could help?' she suggested.

'I could make the notes while you do the assessing.'

He hesitated. For a horrible moment, Ferelith thought that he was going to turn down her offer. But then a smile crossed his face.

'OK. Thanks for that.' He handed her the tablet and she took it, trying not to let the wave of relief she felt show too obviously on her face.

It was simple enough work. Geraint led the way, moving slowly about, stopping here and there to examine a plant or a border or a bush that was looking a bit battered. He would say a few words, Ferelith would key them into the tablet and then they would move on.

In a way, the whole thing was mad. It occurred to her that anyone seeing them would wonder what on earth they were up to at that time of night. But she didn't care. She was with Geraint and that was all that mattered. And as they talked quietly, it felt as if the relationship that had existed between them before was returning.

'There is so much needing done,' she sighed. 'With the artificial snow and the penguins and the concert and the helicopters, the ground is in such a state.'

He frowned. 'It's actually not as bad as it looks. Things do seem a bit knocked about and I wouldn't want the grounds to compete in the Chelsea Flower Show right at the moment. But with a bit of work, the team and I will soon get things back into shape. A month from now and it'll all look completely different. Nature recovers quickly if you give her a chance.'

He was looking at her as he spoke; there was passion in his voice. Her heart began to thud inside her chest. He had gazed at her like that at the concert too. She wondered if this was her chance to speak to him about the confusion which had arisen between them. But somehow it didn't seem to be a time for words. Anyway, he had turned away and the moment was gone.

'The Wishing Well seems to be fine,' he said. She nodded. Sitting on a little table by the circle of shrubs was a plastic box containing a collection of paper stars waiting to be written on, along with a selection of glitter pens. And inside the circle there were lots of Christmas wishes scattered about, some in hoops, some not.

They stood side by side. She was getting cold and she wondered if he might put his arm around her. Then she had an idea. She turned to him.

'Shall we make our own wishes?'

A slow smile spread across his face.

'All right then.'

Opening the box, he held it out to her and she helped herself to a green star and a purple glitter pen. She thought to herself for a moment and then simply wrote *Let him love me*.

Having decorated the words with flowers and bubbles, she folded the star and then folded it again. He was doing the same and she wondered what his message was.

'We don't have the leaf blower; we'll just have to throw them,' he murmured. Ferelith nodded.

'Three — two — one — throw!'

Their paper stars flew into the air, partly unfolding as they did so. They seemed to swirl round and round each other as they fell, as if they were dancing, and landed touching each other in the hoop that said *Your Wish Will Come True!*

★ ★ ★

Ferelith felt her cheeks flush. It was nonsense, of course. But as she looked at Geraint, something in his expression suggested that it wasn't nonsense at all.

This time the silence didn't feel awkward. It was as if they weren't quite sure what was about to happen but yet they knew it would be wonderful.

Dandy Barham drifted into her mind. Pass it on, he had told her.

'Father Christmas gave me a present,' she said to Geraint. She could feel her heart pounding in her ears. From her pocket, she brought out the sprig of mistletoe.

There was a flaring in Geraint's eyes as she lifted it above their heads and, a moment later, their lips came together.

Ferelith thought that she was probably floating. It certainly felt like it as she made her way back into the hotel. She wasn't sure how long she and Geraint had been out in the grounds. They had kissed and kissed and kissed again and said all manner of nonsense to each other, none of which she could now remember. Her whole body was tangled up in a mess of excitement.

She supposed she would be going to bed soon but she couldn't imagine falling asleep; her mind was too full. Geraint was coming back to the Manor in the morning and it was just possible that they might kiss again. One life didn't seem enough for so much happiness.

There were still people mingling about and she found her father by the Christmas tree.

'Hello, Dad,' she murmured with a dozy smile. Lyle was with him. And Franklyn. 'Hello, Lyle. Hello, Franklyn.

Happy Christmas to you all.'

It struck her vaguely that none of them seemed in a very Christmassy mood. In fact, they all had troubled expressions on their faces.

'Is something wrong?'

Though surely it was impossible for anything to be wrong? It was almost Christmas Day and everything in the world was perfect.

'It's the GroupChat phones,' her father said. 'They've disappeared!'

21

'We have to contact the police,' Lionel protested.

'Absolutely not,' Franklyn snapped back. 'In two weeks' time, GroupChat will be carrying out the biggest product launch in the company's history. We've been building up the excitement about this for months. It would be a disaster if news got out that samples of the phones had been released early and were out there somewhere in the hands of goodness knows who. Our entire marketing strategy would be derailed.'

'I have the reputation of the Manor to consider. I can't have people thinking that if they stay at this hotel then their property might be stolen.'

Franklyn looked at him coldly.

'They won't think that if they don't know about it. The police cannot be informed.'

Ferelith couldn't seem to get her mind

working properly. Inside, she was such a mixture of tired and excited and happy and confused.

She looked around the reception area. It was quietening down as people drifted off to their rooms, though there were still quite a few guests lounging around in the armchairs and chatting. They were all adults. The children and young people had been sent off to bed after the party whether they wanted to go or not. It was late on Christmas Eve. They needed a good night's sleep in preparation for the next day's celebrations.

She found it hard to picture what Christmas Day would be like. The staff at the hotel would certainly be kept on the go.

She would be up early for her usual jog, but she had no idea when she would finish her stint. It was bound to be one of those days when her services were con-stantly being called upon. Though that didn't bother her, because there would also be Geraint.

Out by the wishing well, she had let

slip her feelings for him.

'I love you, Geraint,' she had murmured in his ear as his arms held her tight.

He had kissed her forehead, her eyelids, her lips. 'I love you too, sweet Ferelith. I can't think of anything I want more than to spend the rest of my life with you.'

That was what she should be thinking about. She should be cuddled under her duvet with her spare pillow in her arms pretending it was Geraint instead of listening to an increasingly tense discussion between Franklyn and her father about the missing phones.

'We can't talk about this here,' she said, breaking into the argument. 'There are too many people around. Why don't the three of you go to your office, Dad? I'll organise some coffee.'

Lionel nodded. 'Good idea.'

'Bring a bottle of brandy too,' Lyle added with a smile. Unlike Franklyn and Lionel, he didn't seem troubled in the slightest by what was going on. 'We might need it.'

* ★ ★

Poppy behind the bar was wearing a party
hat from a cracker on her head and had
a Christmas badge with flashing lights in
the shape of a star pinned over her heart.

'Are you all set for Christmas, Ferelith?' she asked as she organised the
coffees.

Ferelith looked at her ruefully. 'I
thought I was but now I'm not so sure.'

'Shall I help you carry this?'

'That's all right, I'll manage with a
tray. And maybe you could put a few
of those Christmas dainties on a plate
as well.' They would cheer her dad and
Franklyn up if anything would.

'No problem.'

When Ferelith got to her father's
office, she found the argument still going
strong.

'We're talking about an act of theft
here in the hotel. I can't pretend it hasn't
happened. I'm not prepared to do that.'

There was a determination in her
father's voice which Ferelith hadn't

heard before. He had gone along with so many of Lyle and Franklyn's demands until then. That was the Manor's way. What the guests wanted, the guests got. However, risking damage to the reputation of the hotel was a step too far.

Franklyn had a phone clamped to his ear but he was arguing with Lionel at the same time.

'And we're not prepared to risk derailing the launch of the GroupChat phones. The future of the company depends on their success. We expect to sell tens of millions of pounds worth of product in the first month alone. News of these thefts would be a disaster.'

'But I'm just talking about informing the police, not publishing it all over the newspapers.'

Franklyn just snorted. 'Once you tell even a few people then the news always gets out. When I discovered that the phones had disappeared, I told Lyle. Then he told you. And now you've told your daughter.' Franklyn looked at Ferelith darkly. 'Though that hardly seemed necessary. At the moment, we're the only people who know.'

'Us and the person or people who took them,' Ferelith said quietly.

Franklyn's eyes flashed in irritation. 'Obviously. But we need the situation to stay that way. The fewer people who know, the better.'

'But we can't keep the news just to ourselves,' Ferelith said. 'Every guest in the hotel was given a GroupChat phone. And they were told that their phones could be collected again as soon as the software update was completed.'

Franklyn waved a hand at her in irritation.

'That's no problem. We'll just tell them that there has been another technical hitch. The important question is, what should we do next?'

Ferelith had put the tray down on Lionel's desk.

'Would anyone like a coffee? Perhaps that will help us focus our minds.' *And also reduce the tension in the room*, she thought to herself.

'I'd love a coffee,' Lyle murmured. It had occurred to Ferelith that he was saying very little. It wasn't like him to let others do the talking. His eyes flashed with their usual humour. 'And perhaps one of those Christmas stars. I remember them from when I first arrived at the Manor. They're so delicious.'

Ferelith couldn't help but smile. Lyle turning up on a sleigh with the reindeer seemed to have happened a lifetime ago.

'How was the disappearance of the phones discovered?' she asked as she offered round the dainties.

Franklyn gazed at her sourly as if trying to decide whether her question deserved his attention. 'I went to check them before I retired to my room for the night. I wanted to make sure there hadn't been any problems with the update.'

'That's one of the reasons that I gave out the phones,' Lyle said, taking a sip from his coffee. 'There are always technological glitches with new products. We already knew about the charging problem. But I wanted the phones to be used by ordinary people for a week or so to see if any other issues came to light.'

'And have there been any?'

Lyle shook his head. 'Not as far as I know. I'm pleased with how the test has worked out. The GroupChat phones have been put to good use.'

Ferelith laughed. 'Particularly by some of the younger guests.'

Lyle sat forward, suddenly eager. 'And that was to be expected. It's always young people who take to new technologies first. They're adaptable, curious, willing to try things out. They're the ones who find imaginative ways to put the technologies to use.'

'Whereas older people aren't so keen?' Ferelith suggested.

Lyle shrugged. 'Older people are naturally more conservative. They're willing to use new technologies but only ones with a proven track record and a sound, practical purpose.' He sat back in his seat again with a laugh. 'I wouldn't be surprised if it was the same thousands of years ago when boats were first invented.

The young people jumped into them and sailed off over the horizon to discover what was out there. Meanwhile, the old folk filled them with cabbages and carrots to sell at the market just up the river.'

Ferelith found herself wondering what she would have done. She suspected that it would have depended on whether Geraint was living in the next village or somewhere over the horizon.

'Anyway, I went into the cloakroom where the charger had been set up,' Franklyn interrupted, clearly irritated with the turn that the conversation had taken. 'But it and all the phones were gone. At first, I assumed that Lyle had moved them for some reason. But he knew nothing about it. Someone had stolen them.'

'When do you think that the phones were taken?'

Franklyn shrugged. 'It must have been at some point during the party.'

Ferelith frowned. 'How would that have been possible? There were guests wandering around all over the place. And the reception staff were on duty.'

'That's what I don't understand.'

'One person could have managed it,' Lyle murmured. 'An adult, anyway. Even with all the phones attached, the charger isn't particularly heavy.'

'But it would have been very unwieldy to carry. Erik wouldn't have missed something like that being lugged through the reception area.'

Franklyn's eyes narrowed. 'You would have thought so, wouldn't you? And yet apparently he saw nothing. It's very strange.'

There was a moment of silence. A tinge of anger flushed Lionel's cheeks.

'I hope you're not suggesting that the disappearance of these phones had something to do with the staff of this hotel . . .'

'It would make sense, wouldn't it?' Franklyn retorted. 'There's no reason for any of the guests to have stolen the GroupChat phones; they all had their own phones already. The members of your staff, on the other hand . . .'

'Are completely trustworthy!' Lionel snapped back angrily. Ferelith gazed at him in surprise. Her father was normally the calmest of people; he never lost his temper. 'This hotel has a reputation second to none and that reputation is built on the work of the staff. I can assure you that none of them would ever dream of taking the property of a guest.'

Franklyn wasn't cowed by Lionel's words.

'Perhaps they've been dreaming of the money involved instead. You don't seem to appreciate the value of those phones. To one of our competitors, a GroupChat phone would be worth the earth at the moment. A member of your staff handing it over could name their own price.'

'They wouldn't do that. They have principles.'

'It's amazing how someone's principles can be affected by a handful of banknotes waved in their face.'

Within seconds, a blazing row had blown up between the two men. Ferelith was astonished. But then Lyle was on his feet and hurriedly moving between them before they came to blows.

'Hang on a minute, everyone. Let's calm down a bit. Have you forgotten that it's almost Christmas Day? What would Santa have to say?'

The humour in his voice seemed to ease the situation. Lionel stepped back, looking rather ashamed that he had allowed his feelings to get the better of himself.

'I'm sorry,' he muttered, straightening his tie. 'But I have complete trust in my staff. I don't appreciate them being accused.'

'No one is accusing anyone,' Lyle assured him. 'Neither is there any reason for us to worry about all this. The Group-Chat head of security, Walter Hofmeyer, is perfectly capable of dealing with whatever is going on here. We'll bring him in and he'll get to the bottom of it straight away.'

Franklyn frowned. 'That could be a problem. Walter flew to South Africa two days ago; his plan was to spend Christmas on safari there. He has been informed about the situation but he won't manage to get back here until Boxing Day.'

Lyle grimaced. 'We can't afford to leave it that long. Someone needs to get on top of the things.'

'But who? We can't go to the police. I'm snowed under with work on the launch. And you have your guests to deal with, Lyle.'

The two men turned to Lionel but he held out his hands.

'I have a hotel to run. Tomorrow . . .' He glanced at his watch. '. . . Today is one of our busiest days of the year.'

Silence fell over the room. But then it was broken by Ferelith's hesitant voice.

'What about me? How about if I do a bit of investigating to try and find out what happened?'

22

'Merry Christmas, Ferelith.'

'Merry Christmas, Geraint.'

It was an odd moment. Neither of them seemed to know what to do. Ferelith thought that she would like to throw herself into his arms and kiss him. They had tried that the night before and it had been very successful, she remembered.

She could kiss his lovely lips and his cheeks and his nose and his forehead and his eyelids and his ears. Everywhere, really. And then maybe start back on his lips again.

However, the two of them were standing in the middle of the reception area, and kissing people there wasn't really the done thing. She was sure that Erik wouldn't approve.

So she stared into Geraint's gorgeous eyes instead and blushed at the thoughts that were filling her head.

'It's so nice to see you.' Even as

she said the words, she realised how inadequate they were. It wasn't 'nice' to see Geraint; it was wonderful . . . extraordinary . . . glorious . . . ultra-brilliant . . . hyper-fantastic . . . giga-amazing. Though it wasn't even any of those things. The words hadn't yet been invented to describe how she felt. 'But it's Christmas Day. You shouldn't really be here. You should be having the day off.'

He shrugged. 'I didn't have anything special planned. So I decided to drop by the Manor. There's plenty needing doing to get the grounds back in shape.' A slight flush crept into his cheeks. For a moment, he couldn't seem to meet her eyes. 'And I hoped I might bump into you.'

Oh, please bump into me! The thought rushed into her head.

'I suppose you'll be busy helping look after the guests today,' he said.

The realisation suddenly struck Ferelith. 'Oh my goodness, you don't know about the phones!'

He frowned. 'The phones?'

'It happened last night during the Christmas Eve party; all the GroupChat phones disappeared. They seem to have been stolen. It's caused a terrible fuss.'

Quickly checking to see if Erik was watching, she took Geraint's hand and led him over to a sofa in a quiet corner. They sat down and she held onto his hand — just to ensure that they didn't get separated accidentally — and she told him all about what had happened. 'Franklyn is in such a tizzy. Apparently, it would be utter disaster for the company if their competitors got hold of the phones before the official product launch.'

'Have the police been informed?' Geraint asked. He grinned. 'Maybe we'll have Sergeant Banks and PC Lyons back at the Manor.'

Ferelith shook her head. 'Franklyn won't hear of it. He says that if that happened then word about the theft would almost certainly get out into the media. And that's the last thing they want.'

'So what's going to happen?'

'GroupChat's head of security is going to take charge of the situation. But he's flying back from South Africa and won't arrive here till tomorrow. So in the meantime, I'm going to investigate the matter and see what I can turn up.'

Geraint looked at her in surprise. But then a thoughtful expression fell over his face.

'Maybe I could help?'

Ferelith felt a lurch in her stomach. 'You?'

He shrugged. 'Sorting out the grounds can wait for a day. I could work on the investigation with you instead.'

Ferelith's mind whirled. Spending the day with Geraint. Having him at her side. All the time.

'That would be great.'

A wide smile crossed his face.

'The two of us could become another world-famous crime-busting duo. Holmes and Watson. Starsky and Hutch. Ferelith and Geraint.' His eyes narrowed. 'And if they make a TV series based on our amazing exploits then I insist on you being played by Saoirse Ronan.'

She snuggled a bit closer on the sofa. 'Maybe you could be played by Liam Hemsworth?'

She became distracted by the idea. With a gorgeous couple like Saoirse and Liam as the leads, the stories might involve a fair bit of kissing. Kissing at the start of each episode. Then at the end. Perhaps even from time to time in the middle as well. She gulped and pushed herself to her feet.

'That's something to think about another time. We have an investigation to get on with.'

The two of them were soon focussed on the task in hand. They started by visiting the cloakroom.

'What does this charger look like?' Geraint asked.

'It's about the size of a beachball with lots of leads coming out of it. It was on that table and all the GroupChat phones were plugged into it.'

'It doesn't sound very unobtrusive.'

Ferelith laughed. 'You're right there.

If anyone had tried to carry it through the reception area they would definitely have been spotted.' She went over to the window and grasped the handle.

'Are you thinking that whoever took the charger and the phones might have passed them to someone outside?' Geraint asked.

'That must be a possibility. If the charger didn't leave via reception then it must have been removed from the hotel some other way. Though there's no sign of the window being forced.'

'So perhaps it was an inside job and the theft was carried out by a guest,' Geraint suggested. He frowned. 'Or even a member of staff.'

Their eyes met in a troubled look.

'Neither of those is a very comforting idea,' Ferelith muttered. She thought for a moment. 'Let's speak to Erik. If anyone saw anything suspicious last night, it would have been him.'

★ ★ ★

Erik was clearly shocked at the thought of a serious theft taking place at the Manor.

'I've been racking my brains ever since learned about what had happened,' he said. 'It was a particularly busy night, of course, but the reception area was fairly quiet for most of the time. Everyone was enjoying themselves at the party. Though there were plenty of people milling about before it all started; I could have missed something then.'

Ferelith shook her head. 'Lyle made the announcement about the update at the start of the party. The disappearance of the phones must have taken place after that.'

Erik frowned. 'The next busy time was when the party came to an end. To be honest, things were a bit chaotic then. People were pouring out of the reception room, children were rushing about, everyone was carrying things.'

'So if the person had put the charger and phones in a box then they wouldn't necessarily have been spotted?'

'Perhaps not but if it had been a stranger carrying the box then I would have noticed them,' Erik said. 'I have an antenna for that sort of thing. I'm certain that the only people in the reception area last night were guests and members of staff.' His eyes narrowed. 'And Father Christmas, of course.'

There was a moment of silence.

'You're not suggesting that Dandy might have had something to do with the theft?' Ferelith shook her head. 'Anyway, he was with me after he left the party — apart from when he went to change out of his costume.' She stopped as a sudden thought came to her. 'Though he did that in the cloakroom where the phones were stored.'

The silence between them stretched. Ferelith shook her head.

'I can't believe that Dandy was involved. He was only in the cloakroom for two or three minutes. It would have taken him all that time just to change out of his costume and pack it into the suit bag.'

'The suit bag?' Geraint said. 'Is it possible that . . .'

But Erik had suddenly gasped. 'Goodness, I've just remembered something. We have a display at the reception desk which signals us if any of the alarms around the building go off.'

Ferelith gave a rueful snort. 'Oh, the fun we had with those motion detectors.'

'One did go off at about ten-thirty.'

Ferelith frowned. 'I didn't hear it.'

Erik shook his head. 'The bells only sound in the case of a fire alarm. This was an alarm linked to one of the windows on the ground floor. It lit up on the desk display to show that the window had been opened.'

'Which window?'

'The cloakroom window.' Ferelith gazed at Eric in shock. 'I went to check it, of course, but the window was closed as usual and there didn't seem to be a problem. I assumed that it must have been a false alarm which sometimes happens and I returned to the desk. I'd forgotten all about it until now.'

'But what about the charger and the phones? Were they still there?'

Erik frowned, trying to remember.

'To be honest, my attention was on the window. The party was breaking up and I wanted to get back to the desk as quickly as possible. But I don't recall seeing them.'

Geraint looked at Ferelith uncertainly.

'Is it possible that Dandy opened the window, handed the charger and the phones to someone outside and then locked the window up again?'

'But Dandy's not that sort of person,' Ferelith cried. 'Anyway, how could it have been arranged? No one knew that the phones and the charger were going to be in the cloakroom beforehand apart from Lyle and Franklyn.'

'I suppose there is one way for you to find out,' Erik murmured. 'There's no CCTV in the cloakroom itself but hotel's system does cover the whole of the reception area.'

Ferelith and Geraint caught each other's eyes.

'Let's have a look.'

They hurried into the security room. Geraint sat down at the control desk and began bringing up the CCTV images from the cameras covering reception. Meanwhile, Ferelith was making a call.

'Hi Dandy, it's Ferelith here from the Manor.'

'Merry Christmas, Ferelith!' the fruity voice came down the phone. 'I hope you're enjoying a relaxing day.'

Ferelith just laughed. 'Not exactly.' She explained about the disappearance of the charger and the phones. 'The equipment was in the cloakroom where you changed out of your costume. Do you remember seeing it?'

'I certainly do,' Dandy retorted. 'I thought some alien artefact had arrived from outer space. I kept well away from it, believe me.'

'So it was there when you left the cloakroom?'

'It was indeed.'

Ferelith pulled over a chair and sat down beside Geraint. 'If he had anything to do with the disappearance of those phones then he must be a very good actor,' she muttered. She realised what she had said. 'Which, of course, he is.' But then she noticed the expression on Geraint's face. She frowned. 'Is something the matter?'

'I've been trying to bring up the CCTV footage from the reception area last night,' he said in confusion.

'And?' she prompted him.

'There's nothing there. The data has all been wiped.'

23

Ferelith gazed at the ground. She wasn't sure what she was supposed to be seeing. 'Doesn't it seem odd to you?' Geraint said. 'Why would the window have been opened unless it was to pass the phones and the charger out? Yet there are no marks on the ground at all.'

They were looking at the cloakroom window from the outside of the hotel. A line of pretty Wintersweet shrubs edged the path perhaps half a metre from the wall. Ferelith could see what Geraint meant. The ground between the shrubs and the wall was fairly damp and remnants of the artificial snow were scattered about it. If someone had stood there to collect the charger and the stolen phones, then they would surely have left footmarks of some sort. But the artificial snow looked undisturbed.

'Might the window have been opened so that a message could have been passed

277

to someone?' she suggested.

Geraint's face wrinkled in uncertainty. 'Why take that risk? They must have known that opening the window would raise an alarm.'

'Perhaps the plan was to hand the phones out the window and leave that way but then something stopped them?'

Geraint nodded. 'That's possible. Maybe there were guests wandering about outside getting a breath of fresh air after the party.'

Ferelith frowned. 'But that means the thieves would have had to get the phones out of the hotel through the reception area. And there were people everywhere. A stranger would have been noticed.'

'Unless it wasn't a stranger,' Geraint muttered.

Ferelith looked at him miserably.

'Do you really think the phones might have been stolen by a member of staff or a guest?'

But Geraint didn't look convinced.

'I'm not sure. Why would they do it? We know all the people that work here at the Manor; they're committed to their jobs. And the guests already have Group-Chat phones of their own given to them by Lyle.'

'According to Franklyn, GroupChat's business rivals might have been prepared to pay a small fortune to get their hands on the new phones prior to the big launch. That could have overcome some people's scruples. And then there's the CCTV footage that was wiped from the system. That suggests an inside job.' She let out a groan of frustration. 'We're getting nowhere with this. We need to change our approach.'

She glanced about. They were round the side of the hotel and there was no one to be seen. She moved closer to Geraint. 'Perhaps if you give me a kiss then that will help,' she murmured. He started to laugh but was quickly cut off.

After a while, Ferelith found herself wondering vaguely if it counted as one kiss when it went on for so long but other thoughts got in the way and she didn't come to any conclusion. Eventually, and reluctantly, they moved apart.

'Did it help?' Geraint asked her with a grin.

She nodded. 'I feel a lot better for it.'

He kissed her again, gently and briefly. 'Me too.'

But then she grimaced. 'Though it hasn't got us any further forward with the investigation.' She slipped a hand under his arm. 'Let's go back inside and make a timeline of what happened. Perhaps that will get things a bit clearer in our heads.'

'Good idea.'

They found Holly and Bree sitting together at the top of the steps outside the hotel. 'Hi, girls,' Ferelith said with a smile. 'Merry Christmas.'

'Merry Christmas, Ferelith; Merry Christmas, Geraint,' they replied in unison. Holly's eyes twinkled as she saw the two of them arm in arm. 'I hope all your Christmas wishes are coming true?'

Ferelith felt a blush warming her cheeks. 'They are, as it happens. What are you two up to?'

'We're waiting for the police,' Bree said eagerly.

Ferelith's eyes widened. 'The police?'

'To investigate the disappearance of the phones. We fancy joining the police ourselves one day.'

'I thought you were going to become DJ Klaws's drummer? With Holly on bass guitar?'

Bree shrugged. 'We can do that at the weekends and on bank holidays. But for now, we want to see how the police do their investigation. Maybe we'll be able to provide them with vital pieces of evidence to trap the culprits.'

'It was the penguins!' Holly cried. 'They planned the whole thing.' The girls collapsed into a giggling huddle of penguin noises.

But Ferelith was shaking her head. firmly.

'You're out of luck, I'm afraid. The police aren't being told about the theft. A GroupChat security officer is going to carry out an investigation, though he won't be arriving until tomorrow.'

Holly gazed at her in surprise. 'So nobody is looking into what happened?'

Ferelith smiled at Geraint. 'As it happens, the two of us are on the case. We're seeing what we can find out about it.'

'Not that we've turned up very much so far,' Geraint said ruefully.

'We think it happened last night around the time when the party finished. The phones seem to have disappeared when everyone was milling around. I don't suppose you two saw anything?'

Holly and Bree looked at each other and shook their heads. 'Not really; we were too taken up with our presents,' Holly said. 'I got a mini photo-printer. It's amazing.'

'And I got eight silver earrings based on the planets,' Bree added. She swung her head. 'I'm wearing Saturn and Jupiter today.'

Ferelith gazed at the earrings and felt just a twinge of jealousy that she hadn't been born one of Lyle's relations.

'You are two very lucky girls. But if you do remember anything significant then find us and let us know.'

'We will,' they chorused.

In the security room, Ferelith and Geraint tried to sort out a timeline of events with Geraint typing out the details on the computer keyboard. Though it was rather difficult for him. He could only use one hand as Ferelith was holding tightly onto the other. That slowed them down quite a bit but, having taken hold of his hand, Ferelith was finding that she had lost the power to let go of it.

'I left the party with Dandy Barham at 10.13pm,' she said. 'I remember because I looked at the clock above reception to check the time. And Dandy said that the charger and the phones were still in the cloakroom when he went there to change out of his costume.'

Geraint typed the information out slowly.

'So what happened then?'

Sorting out the timeline did help. There was a clear order of events from Lyle's announcement at the start of the party that all the phones needed to be plugged into the charger to Franklyn's discovery of the phones' disappearance, which had happened by 10.41pm.

Ferelith looked at the screen and shook her head.

'There's one thing that I don't understand. No one knew until the party began that Lyle was going to make an announcement about the phones and insist that they were all plugged into the charger.'

Geraint nodded slowly. 'So it's hard to see how taking the phones could have been planned beforehand?' He looked at her with a troubled expression. 'I can't think of any explanation other than that it was an inside job decided on the spur of the moment.'

Ferelith nodded slowly. 'It's beginning to look like that to me.'

Just then, they heard a kerfuffle outside. Erik looked round the door.

'I have two young guests here who are keen to speak to you. Should I let them in?'

They had no time to answer. Holly and

Bree had already rushed into the room.

'We've thought of something!' Holly said eagerly.

'The man with the beard!' Bree added.

Ferelith raised a hand to Erik to indicate that it was all right. She pulled out two chairs.

'What are you talking about, girls? What man with a beard?'

They answered in a tumble of words.

'He was quite young, maybe in his early twenties.'

'He was wearing a white shirt and black trousers.'

'We thought he was a member of staff; that's what the servers behind the bar wear.'

'What sort of beard?' Ferelith asked.

'Short and ginger,' Holly said confidently. 'And he had a silver stud in his left earlobe.'

Ferelith looked at Geraint with a frown. The description didn't fit any member of staff that she knew.

'Where did you see this man?'

Holly's eyes widened with excitement.

'That's the thing. He was coming out of the cloakroom when we went to plug our phones into the charger. And then Bree saw him later.'

Bree nodded eagerly. 'It was after the party. I thought he was just helping tidy up. He was carrying one of those red bags that Santa's elves had brought the presents in.'

'Was the bag empty?' Ferelith asked.

Bree shook her head. 'There was something in it but I couldn't see what.'

'Could it have been the phone charger and the phones?'

Bree nodded. 'It was that sort of size.'

Ferelith sat back in her seat. At last, they seemed to be getting somewhere.

'The hotel's CCTV should be able to identify him,' Holly said eagerly.

Geraint snorted. 'That's the first thing we thought about. Except that the data from the reception area cameras from last night has been wiped.' His fingers flicked over the keyboard. 'This is all that we have.' He turned the screen and Holly and Bree got to their feet and stood behind Ferelith to look. The screen was a mass of jiggling black and white dots with the occasional fuzzy line drifting across it. 'No young men with ginger beards to be seen there.'

Holly and Bree said their goodbyes. It was Christmas Day and they had plans.

'Enjoy yourselves, girls,' Ferelith called after them and they blew kisses back.

'I want to have a further look at the CCTV system,' Geraint said. 'There may be some useful information stored on it somewhere.'

Ferelith nodded. 'While you're doing that, maybe I'll have a chat to people who were around reception and the cloakroom area last night at the times we're interested in.'

'That's pretty much everyone in the hotel,' Geraint said with a rueful smile. 'Good luck.'

Ferelith started on the task eagerly enough but she found the next couple of hours very frustrating. Although she had no official status when it came to the investigation, most people were happy to talk to her. But what they had to say didn't turn out to be particularly helpful.

Everyone had seen other people carrying packages about. They had all seen guests wandering in and out of the cloakroom. They had all seen children rushing around in excitement. But no one had seen anyone acting in a way which had struck them as unusual. And no one could remember seeing a bearded member of staff carrying a red sack or behaving in a suspicious way.

At the end of it all, Ferelith felt rather deflated. All that talking and there was nothing to show for it. She began to feel some sympathy and fellow-feeling for the police. Cracking major crimes always seemed so easy on television. But perhaps it wasn't such a simple matter.

She decided that it had been far too long since she had last seen Geraint and just the thought of that put a spring in her step. She picked up a couple of coffees and took them through to the security room.

'Break time,' she said brightly. 'And I

grabbed some sweets from the bowl at the bar. How are things going?'

He turned to her, his eyes flickering in excitement. 'Not bad, actually. I've found something rather interesting.'

But Ferelith had become distracted. When she had picked up the sweets, she had dropped them into her bag. As she rustled around to gather them up, she caught sight of something unexpected in her bag. Confused, she lifted it out.

'What on earth . . .'

'A GroupChat phone?' Geraint said in puzzlement. 'Where did that come from?'

'I haven't the faintest idea,' Ferelith retorted. Her eyes widened. 'But it's switched on. And it's on an open line.' She turned to Geraint in shock. 'I'm being bugged!'

24

After the excitement of the Christmas Eve party, the plan at the Manor was to have a rather calmer Christmas Day, though still with a strong sense of festive celebration.

The centrepiece, of course, was the traditional Christmas Day lunch which would finish in time for everyone to listen to the Queen's speech. At the end of it, guests would be invited to stand and toast Her Majesty with something bubbly and then sing a rousing rendition of God Save The Queen.

It would all start with a buffet breakfast available from six for those families with younger children who had woken early in great excitement. A Christmas dinner dance in the evening with a few informal party games would be followed by fireworks before everyone headed off to bed, tired but happy. It was always a wonderful day.

In normal times, the morning of Christmas Day tended to be a relaxed affair. People would exchange festive greetings, of course, but then they would go for walks around the grounds if the weather was suitable or sit about chatting quietly. A few doughty souls would usually join in with the indomitable Miss Buckley-Tone as she played carols on the piano accompanied by members of her church choir.

However, these weren't normal times. There was an atmosphere of high excitement in the reception area with children rushing about and making a racket.

To the amazement of the hotel's staff, Lyle's generosity had extended to providing surprise Christmas gifts for each of them. Ferelith had been given a beautiful set of silver bangles which she adored and Geraint's present was a belt in Italian leather with a bronze buckle in the shape of an oak tree.

Only Erik seemed rather uncertain about his present. He had been given a reindeer tie in mulberry silk which began flashing and playing an electronic version of Jingle Bells whenever anyone nearby was detected saying the word 'Christmas'. He was gamely wearing it but Ferelith thought that she detected a certain look of strain in his eyes.

'So you're getting somewhere with the investigation, Miss Ferelith?' he said.

'We seem to be, Erik, though we're not quite sure where. It's clear that something very strange happened here last night.'

He sighed. 'Strange things have been happening at the Manor ever since the arrival of Mr Cranford and his party.'

Ferelith grinned. 'But it is exciting, isn't it?'

Erik looked around. A cheer had just gone up by the bar at the popping of a cork; a group of guests had ordered Buck's Fizzes all round to wash down their breakfasts. Innumerable children were racing about in a game which seemed to involve climbing over as many pieces of furniture as possible while shrieking at the tops of their voices. Meanwhile, above them all, a drone was quietly circling the chandelier in the centre of the ceiling.

'Excitement can be rather over-rated in my view,' Erik retorted.

Ferelith laughed. 'It is Christmas Day.' At once, Erik's tie started flashing and *Jingle Bells* began to play. His eyes narrowed and Ferelith hurriedly grabbed Geraint's arm and they made their exit.

They stood for a moment outside the entrance of the hotel. There was a chill in the air but it was a glorious day.

'So what's the next step?' Geraint asked.

Ferelith shook her head. 'I'm not sure. I should keep Dad up to date with the state of the investigation. It would be brilliant if we could work out what went on last night before the GroupChat security man arrives tomorrow. It's horrible having a cloud of suspicion hanging over the hotel. But everything is so mixed up at the moment.'

She brought out the GroupChat phone she had found in her bag and looked at it in puzzlement. She had left the line open, though with the microphone switched off so that if there was someone listening at the other end then there would be nothing for them to hear. She wasn't sure what the phone had to tell them but it was their only real clue.

'Do you have any idea when it might have been put into your bag?' Geraint asked.

Ferelith shook her head. 'Not really. I looked through the bag to find my lippy before I left Dad's flat this morning; it wasn't there then.'

'So it must have happened in the last couple of hours?'

'The trouble is that I've been talking to dozens of people. It would have been easy for someone to slip the phone into my bag when I wasn't looking.'

They were standing at the top of the steps. Suddenly, the hotel's doors burst open and two boys rushed out, almost crashing into Geraint and Ferelith.

'Steady now,' Geraint laughed.

'Sorry!' one of the boys said. He

grabbed his friend by the arm. 'Hurry! They're by the pool. I saw them.' The two of them raced off.

Geraint looked after them with a smile. 'Oh for the days when I had that much energy.' But then he noticed the expression of Ferelith's face. She was gazing after the boys with a puzzled look. 'What's the matter?'

'That game they're playing; it's a sort of Hide-And-Seek.'

Geraint nodded. 'The younger guests have been playing it for days. Charging all over the place after each other.'

'But it's not an ordinary Hide-And-Seek. The grounds are too big for that. They've been using their phones to work out where other people are.' She gazed at Geraint. 'Their GroupChat phones.'

Geraint's eyes widened as he realised what she was saying. 'Do you think . . .'

Ferelith nodded determinedly. 'I think!'

Lionel appeared through the doors of the hotel at that moment. His face lit up as he saw her.

'Ferelith, the very person. I've been so busy with everything happening today that I haven't had time to catch up with you. How's it going? Have you managed to make any progress with the investigation?'

Ferelith and Geraint looked at each other.

'It's just possible that we have, Dad.'

She brought her father up to date with what had been happening. He looked at her in confusion.

'Someone dropped a GroupChat phone into your bag so they could hear what you were doing?'

Ferelith nodded. 'That's what it looks like. It must have happened after people realised that Geraint and I were investigating the phones' disappearance. And there's another thing; we think that some of the younger guests at the hotel may be involved.' She told him about the two boys. 'Children have been playing that game for days. And it involves the GroupChat phones.'

Lionel's mouth fell open. 'You think

that they may still have access to them?'

'I do.'

A flash of hope appeared through his worried expression. 'That would certainly be a better outcome than members of staff taking the phones. Or outsiders. So what's your next step?'

Ferelith looked at Geraint. 'I've had an idea about that. If it comes off, it might tell us who was responsible for hiding the phone in my bag.'

Lionel nodded and glanced at his watch.

'I need to go. But it sounds as if you know what you're doing. Let me know how you get on.' He turned and disappeared back into the hotel.

'What's this idea of yours?' Geraint asked.

Ferelith brought out the phone. 'We're assuming that whoever put this into my bag wanted to keep up to date with the state of our investigation. So even though the microphone is off at the moment, they may still be listening in.'

Geraint nodded. 'That makes sense.'

'We're going to make use of that,' she said and she began to explain.

A minute or two later, the two of them made themselves comfortable on one of the benches in the sensory garden. Ferelith looked at Geraint.

'Do you understand what you have to say?'

Geraint nodded. 'I'm ready.'

'Here goes then.' Ferelith unmuted the GroupChat phone and held it between them. She signalled to Geraint with a nod. 'So you know who took the phones?' he said to her eagerly.

'Not yet,' Ferelith replied. 'But we're about to find out. Whoever it was, they left a crucial piece of evidence in the sensory gardens. It's there now. But I think we should tell my father first.'

'I agree.'

'Once we find him, we'll take him to the sensory garden and show him. He'll be so relieved; he's desperate to know who was responsible.'

'He's not the only one. Let's go!'

Ferelith muted the microphone again.

'If anyone was listening in, they're going to be a bit confused. But it should get them jumping into action. Now all we have to do is wait.'

'Fingers crossed that the plan works,' Geraint said. A silence fell between them. He looked at her. 'What should we do in the meantime?' They both had the same idea at the same moment.

We're so perfect for each other, Ferelith thought as their lips met.

A minute or so later, she hurriedly detached herself from his arms, hearing running footsteps.

Holly and Bree burst through the willow arch and came to a sudden, shocked stop.

'Hello, girls,' Ferelith said. She raised an eyebrow. 'Exactly what have you two been up to?'

'It wasn't just us,' Bree cried but Holly grabbed her arm.

'No comment, Bree! That's all we should say.' She gazed at Ferelith, her eyes dark with suspicion. 'We want a lawyer.'

Ferelith's eyes widened. 'A lawyer?'

Holly raised herself to her full height. 'And we demand to see the ambassador!'

The two girls tried to stay silent as they followed Geraint and Ferelith back to the hotel but it was hard for them; they were natural chatterboxes.

'I miss the penguins,' Bree started to say, only to be hurriedly hushed by Holly.

'No comment, Bree!'

Making their way in through the hotel doors, they were spotted by Lionel and Lyle, who were talking by the reception desk. Lyle hurried over.

'Your father has told me you have one of the GroupChat phones?' he said eagerly to Ferelith.

She nodded and handed it to him.

'We now have a pretty clear idea about what happened last night,' she replied, with a glance at Holly and Bree. 'Though we're not sure where the rest of the phones are.'

'I can use this one to find the others,' Lyle said. His fingers flew over the keys. 'I'm putting out a group call to the rest of the phones. Their location beacons will be switched on. Then we'll be able to find them, wherever they are.'

He pressed the call button. A moment later, from across the hall, they heard the sound of dozens of phones starting to ring at the same time. It was coming from one of the large decorated boxes at the foot of the Christmas tree.

★　★　★

Holly and Bree could see the game was up and the whole story quickly came out. As they spoke, a number of other youngsters gathered to add their own contributions. They had all loved their new GroupChat phones but hadn't been so keen on the fact that the phones allowed their parents to keep a close eye on them. When Lyle announced that all the phones would be plugged into the charger during the Christmas Eve party, it gave them the perfect chance to make all their parents' phones disappear.

'There was so much going on after the

party that no one noticed us sneaking the phones and the charger out of the cloakroom in one of the big boxes,' Holly said. 'We'd taken our own phones so we could carry on using them, though we knew we'd have to keep them hidden.'

'Did you wipe the CCTV too?' Ferelith asked.

Holly nodded. 'We opened the window in the cloakroom to set off the alarm. When Erik left the reception desk to check it out, my brother Deke slipped into the security room and cleared the data from the system. He's a total geek.'

'So what about the man with the ginger beard?' Geraint asked in puzzlement.

'We invented him to put you off the scent.'

Lyle burst out laughing. 'Brilliant. I should have guessed.' He held out his hands to the youngsters. 'But there was no need. You could easily set up your own sub-group your parents have no access to. I'll show you.'

'Don't encourage them, Lyle!' one of the adults cried out in mock-horror.

'So you're not angry with us, Uncle Lyle?' Bree asked uncertainly.

'Of course not,' he retorted with a wide smile. 'I gave out the GroupChat phones to see how people would use them. This is exactly the sort of thing I wanted to happen.'

25

'I just don't like surprises,' Lionel said wearily. 'Especially ones involving Lyle Cranford.' Ferelith burst out laughing; the look on her father's face was a picture.

'Whatever Lyle's surprise is, it can't be that bad. He and his guests will all have left the hotel in a couple of hours.'

However, Lionel didn't look convinced. The past few days seemed to have passed in a blur for Ferelith. With Lyle and his guests around, the hotel's staff were always going to kept on their toes. But after the mystery of the phones was solved, no further disasters or emergencies had occurred. Everyone seemed to have enjoyed a brilliant Christmas and Lionel had felt that, all in all, it was a job well done. He had almost begun to relax. Until Lyle had announced to the guests at breakfast that morning that he had arranged one last surprise before they left the Manor. All would be revealed at ten that morning.

'I suppose I'll cope,' Lionel said with a sigh.

'How are the bookings looking for when Lyle's party leaves?' Ferelith asked.

Lionel's face brightened. 'Not bad at all.' His fingers flicked over his keyboard and he gazed at the screen. 'We're over 90% full for our New Year celebration package. And we always pick up a few last-minute bookings for that.' He turned to her with an expression of wonder. 'Can you imagine it? A hotel full of normal guests.'

The reception area was a bustle of activity. Lyle had asked people to gather outside the hotel for the surprise and, though it was still a bit early, there was a distinct buzz of excitement in the air.

'Hi, Ferelith!'

'Do you know what the surprise is?'

'Are the penguins coming back?'

'Is DJ Klaws doing a farewell concert?'

It seemed to Ferelith as if, whenever Holly and Bree appeared, a whirlwind accompanied them. Their question all came in a rush with the two girls dancing around her. She shook her head. 'Sorry, girls. I'm as much in the dark as you.'

'Ooooh,' they cried in disappointment, but they were already racing off and out of the hotel.

She slipped behind the reception desk. 'Have you heard there's going to be a surprise, Erik?'

He closed his eyes momentarily. 'I shudder to think what it might be, Miss Ferelith.'

'Is there anything I can do to help in the meantime?'

'If you could assist in manning the phones then that would be a great boon. With the guests all leaving together, there will no doubt be a rush of calls for assistance of one sort or another.' He frowned. 'Though before you sit down, could you take a message to Geraint?'

A sizzle of pleasure went through Ferelith. She'd seen Geraint earlier. Somehow, the two of them managed to find their way to each other whenever he arrived for work each morning. But the thought of seeing him again made her smile and blush at the same time.

'Could you ask if he and his team could assist the porters when the guests start to leave?'

'Of course. I'll do that now.'

She made her way through the hotel doors and realised there really was a song in her heart. It was like a tumult of birds swooping about singing, 'My love! My love! I'm going to see my love!' for all they were worth. It left her feeling rather breathless.

Geraint was with Faisal and the two of them were looking thoughtfully at a flower bed. 'I'm surprised how quickly the artificial snow has disappeared,' Geraint was saying. 'The worms really have taken to it.'

Faisal nodded. 'We should have the grounds back in shape fairly quickly.'

They turned to her and Ferelith resisted the urge to throw herself into Geraint's arms and kiss him all over his perfectly gorgeous face.

'I have a message from Erik. Could you and the team help the porters with the luggage when the guests start to leave?'

'No problem.' Geraint looked at Ferelith curiously. 'What do you think this surprise of Lyle's is going to be?'

Ferelith laughed. 'I haven't a clue.'

'I'm not sure I want to find out,' he said ruefully.

'Oh I don't know. Surprises can be interesting,' she murmured. She looked at him and he looked right back at her. Time seemed to stop.

Faisal cleared his throat. 'Right, I'll go and . . . and . . .' He didn't seem sure what he was going to do but he was clearly leaving. 'See you two later.'

He hurried off and the corners of Ferelith's mouth twitched in a smile. 'Faisal is really quite a thoughtful person,' she said. But Geraint had already taken her by the hand and was pulling her gently behind the oak tree.

'I've missed you so much,' he growled and Ferelith's peal of laughter was cut short as she found herself being thoroughly kissed.

Ferelith became vaguely aware of people gathering noisily in the distance but she hardly noticed; she had other things to concentrate on. It was only when a cheer rose up, accompanied by enthusiastic whistles and whoops, that the two of them eventually separated.

They looked round the oak tree to see what was happening. Ferelith's mouth sagged open. 'I don't believe it,' she whispered.

★ ★ ★

'I suppose it's another skill to add to my acting CV,' Dandy said to Ferelith. 'The day might come when I'm required to ride a camel on stage.' He was dressed in a glorious costume of azure silk. His outrageous headgear and luxurious slippers with curled-up toes only added to the effect.

There was a shriek. The guests surrounding the three camels were scattering; one of the animals had decided it was a good time to relieve itself.

Dandy raised an eyebrow. 'I suppose it will be good for the roses.'

'I couldn't believe it when I saw you and your fellow actors coming up the drive,' Ferelith laughed. 'You were swaying about so much on the camels I was sure you were going to fall off.'

Dandy held his arms out in a dramatic pose. 'The Three Kings have arrived bearing gifts from afar!' he cried. 'Well from Harrods, probably.'

Each camel had been led by a handler, also gloriously dressed, with half a dozen servants following carrying bags of going-away presents which the kings had distributed. For the guests, it had been an amazing end to an amazing stay.

'I'm sure I noticed you canoodling with a young man as I was coming up the drive,' Dandy murmured. 'Can I assume that he was the subject of your aching heart when last we met?'

Ferelith felt suddenly so full of feeling that she could barely speak. 'He was, Dandy.'

'And can I also assume that things are going well for the two of you now?'

Ferelith nodded. 'Your gift worked perfectly.'

'I'm glad, my dear. If there's one thing I've learned from a long and varied life it's that, when you find love, you must cling to it.'

★　★　★

Dandy had gone, the camels had gone and so had virtually all the guests. Ferelith got wearily to her feet and stretched. As expected, the internal phonelines had been going non-stop with queries and requests. She had been kept continuously busy, though the final call had made her smile. The light had lit up on the panel and she had pressed the button. 'How may I help you?'

'Is that Ferelith?'

Ferelith frowned. The voice sounded familiar.

'It is.'

'We have a complaint!' There were

giggles at the other end of the line.

'I'm sorry to hear that. May I know the nature of it?'

Holly and Bree's heads popped up from the other side of the reception desk, Holly's phone pressed against her ear. 'It's not fair; we want to stay another week!' they shouted together. 'We had such a good time. Thank you, Ferelith!'

'Bye, girls,' she called but they were already rushing off, the last of the guests to leave.

Calm descended over the reception area, now empty apart from the staff clearing up. It was broken only by the gentle notes being played by Miss Buckley-Tone on the piano. Erik placed his palms flat on the reception desk and took a long, slow breath. 'Perhaps we can look on the whole extraordinary episode as a nightmare which is now blessedly over,' he said in fervent tones.

Ferelith was still grinning as she made her way outside. She found her father standing with Lyle at the top of the steps.

'I know that the hotel's grounds have

taken a bit of a hammering over the past week or so,' Lyle was saying. 'My plan is to add an extra something on top of my bill which should help Geraint get things quickly back into shape.'

Lionel's eyes widened in surprise.

'That's very kind of you, Mr Cranford.'

Ferelith agreed, but she felt that it was typical of Lyle. He was a generous man. The sum he had mentioned was bound to be a significant one.

However, Lyle just waved a dismissive hand.

'Not at all. It has been worth every penny. We've all had a wonderful time at the Manor.'

'I'm glad to hear it.'

'In fact, we've enjoyed ourselves so much, I've decided to book up the whole hotel again at Easter.'

Ferelith had to turn away before she burst out laughing. The always polite expression on her father's face had looked as if it was straining to contain a tidal wave of horror.

She found Geraint under the oak tree reaching up to detach the last of the fairy lights. Not caring if anyone was looking, she slipped her arms round his waist and squeezed his lovely body.

'What's that for?' he asked in amusement.

'I was talking to one of the three kings,' Ferelith murmured. 'He said that if I ever found love then I should hold onto it tightly. I intend to do just that.'

Geraint returned the hug, which was a very kind thought, Ferelith felt, and when he kissed her, after a moment she kissed him right back. It seemed the polite thing to do, and she had always been a well-mannered girl.

We do hope that you have enjoyed reading this large print book.

Did you know that all of our titles are available for purchase?

We publish a wide range of high quality large print books including:
Romances, Mysteries, Classics
General Fiction
Non Fiction and Westerns

Special interest titles available in large print are:
The Little Oxford Dictionary
Music Book, Song Book
Hymn Book, Service Book

Also available from us courtesy of Oxford University Press:
Young Readers' Dictionary
(large print edition)
Young Readers' Thesaurus
(large print edition)

For further information or a free brochure, please contact us at:
Ulverscroft Large Print Books Ltd.,
The Green, Bradgate Road, Anstey,
Leicester, LE7 7FU, England.
Tel: (00 44) **0116 236 4325**
Fax: (00 44) **0116 234 0205**

DOLPHIN'S KISS

Dawn Knox

Growing up in Sydney in the early 1800s, Abigail Moran knows only the constraints of a privileged life, and that she must hide the birthmark on her left hand at all costs. Yet the mark might prove to be the key that unlocks the secrets of her turbulent start in life aboard a convict ship — and, on a very different boat trip, it could open her eyes to real love . . .

THE COWBOY'S TREASURE

Jill Barry

Katie is a young governess who leaves Yorkshire to take over her aunt's teaching post at a small country town school in America. Not long after she arrives, she meets Ben, a young cattleman who is also new in town. On riding in, Ben had happened upon an old man who had been attacked. Although unable to keep the stranger alive, he learned a secret from him: one linked to Katie's aunt . . .